PRAY OR BE PREY

AMAZON BESTSELLER

ZITA GRANT

This is a work of fiction. Names, characters, businesses, places, events and incidents either are the products of the author's imagination or used in a fictitious manner. Any resemblance to actual persons, living or dead, or actual events is purely coincidental.

Printed in the United States of America
ISBN 978-1-945491-27-6

Published by 2 Tigers LLC

The first edition

CONTENTS

Ayularc

CHAPTER 1

Eyes flashed open, trying to focus, to determine dream from reality. There was nearly no light in the space except for a low orange glow in the far left corner of the room. Its source was that of a small nightlight. Tiny hairs on the ears danced as airflow streamed from the ceiling fan above. Taking in the immediate surroundings and the goosebumps now forming over bare arms, the brain concluded it was registering the tangible. A pair of medium-light brown eyes were shuttered again as the brain did it's best to recall the events of the night. Vivid events. The images were in color, their brilliance undeniable, many of which the tones, proved to be a challenge for the brain place—their luminescence beyond the vocabulary it possessed. There was someone tall—a man, male for sure. A man was the closest reference, though it lacked so much when considering many of his—its characteristics. His hair was the one image that stayed at the forefront of the memory. It was mesmerizing.

Another memory washed away the current one with a backdrop of black sky. Very few lights of the night sparkled against it. Only something like that of gunmetal grey outlined an aircraft of sorts. Its appearance was not like any aircraft known to exist. There was no tail or long wingspan. This ship was shaped more like that of an oblong piece belonging to a child's shape-learning toy set. It had rows of lights near the top, while the underneath was solid grey. Silently it sat, suspended in the air. After a few moments, the aircraft slowly began to move towards what one would describe as a tear in the sky. As if someone or something had pulled down a zipper because on the other side of the slit shone a bright yellow, almost white light.

The brain continued to try and recall more of the dream but wasn't successful. Instead, it let the darkness envelope it until consciousness conceded to the lure of slumbering bliss. Sending out one last instruction, the body turned on its left side while pulling the cool sheet over the right shoulder. Mirah's lungs expanded to their limit before forcing the air out of her mouth. Head nuzzling deeper into the fluffy pillow. She slept well into the early hours of the morning, unaware that her dreams were much more than nighttime entertainment. They held keys to the days and events which soon would invade her reality. That was six months ago.

⌘⌘⌘⌘⌘⌘

Dew hung like a thick blanket while the pair made their way as quietly as possible through the remaining stretch of tall grass, which ended at the river's edge. Father and son, both tired and cold from the long night's journey, picked up the pace sensing hope just beyond the far sides embankment. Fog appeared to levitate over the calm waters, making visibility much less than the father had hoped at this time of the morning.

Flickering rays from the new day's sun creeping across the horizon fought to push through small openings of the dark—nearly black clouds which had begun to remain in the skies as of fifteen days ago. These were no ordinary clouds; they didn't move in the air—always stationary—menacing. At first, the weatherman on the TV advised everyone that they appeared to be stationary clouds, when in fact they were moving slower than human eyes or current technology could detect. Still, after five days, panic started to bubble through the city, threatening to erupt like a too long-dormant volcano. Something was very wrong. The undeniable fact coursed like shocking electricity through people's veins.

It was by the eighth day that pockets of chaos spewed without much resistance into the streets. The almost constant overcast sky, lack of daylight, and skin prickling fear were taking their toll on everyone. Residents began to raid the grocery stores, turning into looting as the days went by. Not long after that, there was a run on the banks. First responders became overwhelmed. People started to stay home, adults not going to work, children not going to school. It was as if an apocalyptic movie was being played out. Anyone in their right mind could tell, whatever was taking place, humankind was not the cause of it. It was evident that staying in the city was no longer becoming a safe option.

The father unpacked the inflatable raft from his backpack, with his eyes scouring the horizon as it self inflated—hairs on the back of his neck sensing the slightest change in the air. Surprised yet glad that they had not come across anyone else, he gave his son an assuring hug. Then quietly as he could, he positioned them both on to what was hoped to provide their passage to safety.

Halfway across the river, now surrounded in the dense fog, a loud boom sound almost made them capsize. Holding each other tight while trying to figure out where the noise was coming from, a child's voice was heard whispering above the gentle lapping of the river's waters on the raft.

"Papa, what was that? Was that a giant sea monster coming to eat us?"

"No, son. It was probably coming from the city we left behind. Sounded like a power transformer blowing up—no need to worry. Just hold onto me; we're almost to the other side," the father said as reassuring as his voice would allow. He swallowed hard to push down the sudden bile clawing at his throat while he tried to steady his racing heart.

Without warning, they were encased by what appeared to be a circular rubber tube that had descended from the clouded sky directly above. Before they could get their wits about them, the pair felt themselves being pulled up. Clinging again tighter to each other, the father looked below to see the river and their raft becoming smaller and smaller—barely illuminated by some light source they were approaching that was casting eerie shadows.

"Lord Jesus help us!" was all the father could manage to say before their mouths were forced closed by pressure from what felt like a hand—but there was no one else ascending with them.

⌘⌘⌘⌘⌘⌘

Mirah walked into the game arcade and dinner; the mixed scent of cooking grease, loud perfume, and cigarette smoke nearly choked her. A handful of people played arcade games with slightly more scattered around the dinner section, lost in conversation while devouring the food before them. Interestingly all the food they were eating seemed a bit on the uncooked side. None of which, save a few odd faced ones, paid her any attention. As Mirah walked along the space between the gaming area and dining tables, she was approached by, assumedly, a manager overdressed in a charcoal gray suit and crisp white shirt. His unnaturally wide smile put her off a bit—it looked like a plastic surgery job gone horribly wrong. He motioned for her to follow him further into the space near the back.

They passed through a set of double doors, opening to a dimly lit hallway lined with rooms on either side. Gone was the prior loaded air she was forced to inhale, replaced now by that of a mixture of sweat, urine, mold, and cleaning chemicals. Mirah's breakfast violently spring-boarded then swan-dived in her stomach. Sprays of its contents threatened to add to the sparsely decorated walls along the corridor. Taking a deep breath, she gulped and pushed down the pending onslaught, pressing her midsection as she walked.

The space was nearly deadly silent, all for the low moans escaping from behind half-opened doors, broken by an occasional scream which was quickly silenced with the sound of a thud. While passing each room, Mirah stole a peek inside only to see people laid on surgical tables. Arms, legs, and heads kept in place by black velcro bands. Trying to remain calm, she took another long deep breath reassuring herself she would make it out of this sudden nightmare alive. Mirah was, after all, a well-known reporter, and if she ended up missing, there were measures in place making sure the guilty would pay.

The manager stopped at the end of the hall; the clicking of his shoe heels echoed off the nearby wall. He fully turned then extended his left hand, directing Mirah into a room. Yellowish lumination came from a tall floor lamp at her right in the farthest part of the space. The wall at her left was covered in a maze of steel pipes and clear plastic tubes. The one on the right was three quarters taken up by a huge mirror. Mirah expected it was a two-way one because she could sense more than one pair of eyes raking across her body from behind it. *I've investigated some creepy places, but this place is a thousand ways more creepy!* Her mind whispered.

"Ahh, there you are. So glad you could come."

Mirah's attention was pulled from the mirror back toward the left wall. *That voice, I know it. Where from, is the question.* She now noticed the black curtain drawn across the side opposite the door, once hidden by the dark shadow just outside the reach of the lamp's light. It was from behind that curtain the man, at least she thought him to be, had slowly appeared. She gathered he had to have been at least 6' 5"—from her use of the door's height in a mental assessment. He was relatively thin with long limbs and unusually long fingers. His hair was straight flaxen; it seemed to almost glow within the faint light of the lamp. Light-colored tendrils fell past his shoulders by three inches or so, and his eyes—like none she could recall. They had a slight almond shape, but not like those of any Asian she was aware of. Their irises were also larger than usual, having a dark brown almost black appearance with a thin ring of yellow-gold around the outer edge. He held her gaze for an uncomfortably long time. His presence was overpowering the space, so much so that Mirah was sure she felt her body vibrating from his nearness.

"The tip or should I say invite received made it sound too good to pass up."

"Yes, I'm sure it got the better of your curiosity. Just as you have gotten ours," the tall man responded, still holding her gaze.

With a swift move of his left arm, the black curtain was drawn aside. What Mirah saw almost made her knees give way. Managing to steady herself, she slowly took in the sight. Strapped to a T-shaped table was a man stripped down to his underwear. Arms stretched out wide, with fists clenching, trying to break free. Unlike the others she had witnessed in the rooms prior to arriving at this one, this man's head was not bound.

Swallowing hard, Mirah was able to formulate her thoughts. "Just exactly what is it you people are doing here? Why do I get the feeling that none of this is legal?"

"What we are doing here is working to save the world. With that intention, we are not concerned with any legality—not the legality that is, which you are referring to."

"Then why take a chance and invite me here? You do know that I'm a reporter for one of the biggest newspapers in the city?"

"Your life as is a reporter is of no concern to us."

"Oh? Then what about my life, precisely, is a concern to you?"

"Your dreams. The ability you have to see beyond the veil that separates your world and ours."

Unsure as to what this man or whatever it was had just alluded to, Mirah took another look around the room. Something just seemed off. She could certainly feel the floor beneath her feet, smell the mixture of blood, alcohol, and some other chemicals she just could not put her finger on. Still, the uneasy feeling lingered regarding the whole situation. *Nope, this can't be one of my dreams! But if this is not a dream...*

"We'd like for you to take a look at these schematics," the blonde-haired man said, pointing to the mirror behind her, cutting off Mirah's racing thoughts.

Turning, Mirah saw that the mirror now had an overlay of almost neon blue engineering drawings in front of it—no, not an overlay but projecting from it in 3D. She reached out to touch a blue line, only to have her fingers move through it, displacing the image momentarily, causing her to let out a gasp.

"Why show these to me? I'm no engineer. And just how are you doing this? I mean, we have emerging tech all the time, but this is some top-level..."

"Never mind the tech involved, concentrate on the design," Blondie said, his tone of voice now more stern, the previous honey edges seared away from his words.

"As I said, I'm no engineer. These mean nothing to me," Mirah replied, matching his tone, inwardly saying a quick prayer of protection from whatever it is she'd gotten herself mixed up in. "Look, I don't know what's going on here, and if you haven't noticed, something is certainly happening in our skies. Unless you have information about that, I'm out of here."

"Oh, I have information about that. Lots of information. However, in exchange for insight into what's going on outside, we will require your assistance in meeting the demands for more of our, shall we say, volunteers."

By this time, Blondie's eyes were fixated on the man strapped to the T-shaped table. A cold chill ran up Mirah's back while the air from her lungs was almost simultaneously sucked out. Still puzzled about what was taking place, she looked back-and-forth between the three others in the room.

"Come now, don't tell me you haven't figured it out yet? Very well, let me break it down. Behind you are schematics for water and land vehicles, robotics of a sort. Like anything mechanical, there must be a power source. Here is one of our gracious volunteers—Bob. Behind me on this wall are pipes and tubes used to obtain that needed power source. Essentially draining Bob, I mean our volunteer. Problem is, eventually our volunteers need to be replaced as they, how can I put this," he continued placing the index finger of his left hand to the corner of his broad grin; long tipped teeth exposed, "run dry!"

Upon hearing this, Bob began to squirm, his eyes bulging from their sockets, terror contorting his face. Try as he might to free himself, his mouth only remained opened as his screams went unheard. As if something was stealing their sound away. Without warning, a huge needle sunk into the base of his neck. Body going rigid upon impact, while tears flowed from his fixed gaze. Bob's blood quickly began to fill up the clear plastic tubes, then pipes along the wall. Unable to move, frozen, Mirah stood there with eyes glued on the horrific sight. She watched, as with each of her breaths, the life of Bob slipping away until his pupils became fully dilated.

"Why me? There are other reporters or dreamers you could've called," Mirah finally managed to say with her mouth now dry from trying to suck air into her lungs. A desperate attempt to ward off the sensation of fainting.

“True, but not all of them can hear us. It takes a special kind of, shall we say, belief? You, dear Mirah, are, without a doubt, one of the easiest for us to mentally reach.”

Mirah replayed the events which brought her to this moment. Try as she may, she couldn’t remember anything prior to setting foot through the front door of this place. Slowly she took in the room where she stood. The blond-haired man before her, the manager still stationary just inside the threshold, the wall of pipes and tubes, even the man on the T-shaped table—Bob, began to appear now slightly out of focus. This awareness was something she had felt before, something that had recently become all too familiar.

“This isn't real,” she said softly. Then with certainty, Mirah shouted, “this isn't happening!”

“Oh, this is real, and it is happening. You just are not, Hmmm, all here.”

“The last thing I remember was watching the late-night news on my sofa. Then I was walking in the front door of this place. Nothing in between. This is a dream!”

“Mirah, Mirah, Mirah. This is not a dream,” Blondie insisted.

“Yes, it is! And I understand the significance of the dream world. Everything and anything that I come into agreement with will manifest in the physical world. Hmmm, so that's why you wanted me to agree to help you get, what did you call them—volunteers? No, I won't do it. I will not be a part of your evil schemes."

"You—my dear—have no choice. We are running out of time. We must have blood!"

"Yeah, right. Because *your world* depends on it. Well, my world depends on me not agreeing with you. I have no doubt you have something to do with what's going on in the skies, and everything you showed me here confirms it. Now I know, and soon the rest of the world will too. They will all know just what is really going on behind the scenes. Everything in the past few days has been nothing but a diversion. While people are busy fighting and scavenging in the streets, you've been rounding up volunteers. No one would certainly miss people with all the chaos that's going on. Everyone's too busy just trying to survive."

"You've always been a smart one, Mirah. We know if we can get people like you on our side, taking over this world would be much easier. Nevertheless, we have other means to get our goals accomplished; others who are willing as well as blinded to the truth."

"I come against any covenant I've made in this dream that was not with God, The Most High. I plead the Blood of Jesus over every scheme of yours. I called down the Fire of Heaven to burn this place to the ground and all those you have around the world harvesting the blood of humans and..."

Before Mirah could say another word, she woke up on her sofa. Remaining still, she blinked hard and took in her surroundings. The sounds of car metal smashing together and sirens blaring in the distance confirmed she was indeed awake. The taste of iron from blood in her mouth seconded it. During her dream, she must have bitten her tongue. Sitting up, eyes focusing on the TV screen, she listened as the reporter issued a statement urging everyone to be cautious on the streets, to remain indoors as much as possible.

The pounding in her chest made her groan. Rubbing her temples, Mirah tried to slow down her pulse. *Slow and deep breaths, that's it.* Everything will be fine; there is nothing to panic over. *Hmmm, that must have been some dream, but for the life of me, I can't remember what it was about. Must have been important because the enemy has wiped my memory clean.* Chimes rang out from her cell phone. The screen displayed a meeting reminder. She had thirty minutes before her video conference with the team from work. She glanced to her left to see notepapers littering the nearby desk she used for work.

"Come on, girl, you have just enough time to grab some coffee and detangle this bird's nest you call hair," Mirah encouraged herself, speaking out loud.

CHAPTER 2

Six hundred years. Not a relatively long time for us, but still, it was long enough for many to become agitated at the snail's pace this project was taking. Our fathers had searched everywhere for remnants of us to the point many had lost hope. Thankfully, a few pressed on, knowing somewhere, hidden, samples of our DNA survived. The Deluge had completely covered the earth killing all life.

All life, save those that the handmade ark secured. We climbed the tallest buildings, trees, and mountains available to us, while the humans scurried around like rats—clawing their way to the highest heights. Countless, though, had become like ants, squished under our huge feet. I was one of the few to remain until the end. My love and four others from our city had managed to make it to the tallest mountain in the land. Finding shelter there from the neverending water that fell from the skies, we were sure our lives would be spared. Spared the fate of all we'd known, built, cultivated. That surety was short-lived, evident by the fifth day.

I held my love as tight as my sore arms could. The current of the water which had nearly flooded the shallow cave snatched her from my grip without warning. Her horror-filled eyes were the last I remember as water muffled her screams. Shortly after, I gave up hope. There was no need to delay my fate. With one last look over the wave cresting horizon, I took my last breath as another push of the current thrust me against the jagged stone walls. Piercing pain on the right side of my neck, then nothing. No pain, not shivering or warm flesh, only an unquenchable thirst to feel, touch, breath again, to live. My kind wandered the earth for hundreds of lifetimes. But it was not the earth as we knew it. It was a place we called The Void. There we were to never find rest, peace, or pleasure.

Then, by some miracle, our fathers found the cave. But instead of it being high above the clouds as on that dreadful day, it was only 13,000 feet from the ground. That meant that much of the earth's surface had been changed by the strong currents of the flood. Some of my DNA had survived, trapped in an air pocket behind some rocks. How it did, none could understand, only elated it had. Once the knowledge of the retrieval of my DNA had become widespread, a renewed determination to find that of others ensued.

For several hundred years, a viable host body was sought. Every experiment showed more promise than those prior. Still, none had the complex makeup needed for the modifications our fathers did to us. No longer did they want us to be the giants of old. In order to continue their agenda, we had to walk freely amongst humans. We had to act, walk, speak—look human.

For over two hundred years, I infiltrated societies, recruiting humans to obtain them for what our fathers had soon come to realize. Sourcing human blood. Just as it is the lifeforce for humans, it had proven to be the life source for our ultimate army. The DNA pool of my kind was limited. There wasn't enough to produce the numbers we once had. Procreation was still tricky since the males, after reaching adulthood, proved to be sterile. Only a few of our fathers volunteered to mate again with human women, hoping to produce females for us to mate with. But of every hundred newborns, only about five were females, and they too were sterile. A cruel punishment and reminder, no doubt by The Most High. He had intended our kind to be killed off by the waters. Our attempts to reclaim the earth as before would not be granted to us so easily.

Out of determination and need, the innovation of our metallic army formed. The metal was forged using ancient understandings, lost to mankind, but not to our fathers. These machines could contain the spirits of the newborns who often didn't survive their first six months of life. Again, defects in the DNA from over cross-breeding. Yet, their spirits roamed, confused and afraid in The Void. Such innocence was easy to mold to the plan. Once they experienced the freedom and security of the metallic shell, they quickly integrated with it, hungering only for human blood to sustain its circuitry's functionality.

However, this wasn't the only reason we needed humans. We'd be able to use not only their blood but also their bodies to help construct the bodies many of the older spirits required to live in the physical world. Such was my side interest. I'd become practically obsessed with perfecting the process currently used. Efficiency among my kind was something well praised and rewarded—the rewards for me were motivation enough!

My job's objective was clear. Continue to provide humans (volunteers) to be used in the blood banks we had scattered all over the earth. Watch out for any human who could hear, sense, or see us (yes, they do exist). Most importantly, don't get captured by any government agency. The majority were under our control, but within the past 80 years, shadow governments have been on the rise. These were more difficult to infiltrate.

Currently, I've set up shop in an average-sized city along the east coast of the USA. The large number of people passing through provides great cover should they go missing. Besides that, the local crime element has not only become a great source of fresh volunteers, but a small business proposition made with the leaders has proven quite beneficial for all involved. They provide disposal of whatever remains of our volunteers; we periodically give them new formulas for product to sell on the streets. The rivalry amongst the gangs to be the one with the latest formula keeps our activity how we like it, a secret.

Are you there, Ayularc?

I'm here, Ayularc replied, lips not moving.

What is the status with the latest delivery?

On schedule. We will be ready for the transport team at the designated location and time, this Friday.

Noted!

After a few moments of silence and feeling the pressure subside in his head, Ayularc let his shoulders relax. To hear his name spoken in his native language always seemed out of place lately. The humans he did business with had many names for him, yet none came close to his real one. Not that they'd know it. No human for many generations had spoken it or understood how, before the flood, to utter his name could mean death. In his previous life, he was feared by many humans and his own kind. But those were different times which called for such ruthlessness. The world had progressed into a place where a softer yet firm hand and beguiling smile proved more effective.

Ayularc turned his focus back to the laptop screen on his desk. He'd been mindlessly surfing the Internet when his thoughts had drifted back to a life long lost. It had been triggered by a video of people enjoying a day out on a boat fishing and drinking. Laughter rang from their lips; they were carefree. Carefree and oblivious to what was about to peel back the smiles off of their faces, switching out the joy in their eyes for that of awe and fright. The right corner of Ayularc's mouth tilted up as he relished the thought of draining each of them.

"Happy, silly rats," he whispered to the laptop screen.

CHAPTER 3

Bed sheets were a crumbled mess, half hanging off the foot of the bed. A few decorative bed pillows had found their way a few feet from Mirah on the bedroom floor. It was still hours away from sunrise, but to Mirah, the warm caress of sun rays kept her connected to the visions before her. Restlessly her body tossed, appendages shifting, trying to find a comfortable position.

The vision continued. People walked past her on a crowded sidewalk. Some were going in and out of storefronts. The street looked familiar, but she was not quite able to place it. The flash of someone just up ahead spurred her forward, almost unobserving of the obstacle course consisting of bodies and store signs in her way. *There, to the right. That hair and profile. I know them. I'm sure I do! Mirah continued on for a little while longer until spotting a man crossing the street, weaving between moving traffic. He was fast, unusually so.* Abruptly, her forward momentum stopped as if hitting an invisible wall. Standing now on the other side of the street, just outside the front door of a café, *he* stood. Eye contact unmistakable as she held her breath. Those eyes, deep and endless, filleting her soul. Again, the corner of his mouth turned up, displaying a taunting little smile. *Mr. Blondie!*

Then with a blink, she was no longer on the sidewalk. Instead, her view was from high above. Higher than she had ever been in her life. A cave, she was standing at the mouth of a cave. Water—everywhere covered in raging water. The sky was like a marble kaleidoscope of grey and black hues as rain fell forcefully, pelting all in its path without mercy. She raised her left arm to shield her eyes from the onslaught, gasping at the sight of it. The arm was not hers! Eyes snapped to her torso, legs, fingers reaching for her face, hair. *What in the world? What is happening to me, my body? Where am I?* Her questioning thoughts elevated in pitch and loudness in her head. Before she could think of another question, a voice bellowed from a space deep in the back of her mind.

"HOW DID YOU GET HERE?" The voice was so forceful; it vibrated through her ears.

With a jolt, Mirah sat up in her bed. The bedroom had become illuminated by the dawn, creeping its way over her neighboring building's roof through the double window on the far right wall. The usual sounds of the neighborhood confirmed she was indeed awake, at home, in her bed! Both hands quickly ran over her body, face, then hair. Satisfied she was herself and no one else, she let her body fall back on the bed. Aimlessly she reached for an extra pillow, propping herself against the headboard, doing her best to replay what was the wildest dream she'd had in a very long time.

"Okay, I was following someone, ahhh yes that man from the other night's dream. Weird room, machine schematics, blood, humans. Mr. Blondie!" She said just above a whisper. "Now, why was I following you? Hmmm. Wait, he saw me. But it was more like he looked right through me, inside me—a café! Yes, there was a café. It looked familiar, but I just can't place the street. And how in the world did he zig-zag through traffic like that? Water. Lots and lots of water everywhere. Then, OH MY GOD! Why was my consciousness in another body? Whose body was it? Was it their voice that almost deafened me? Arrrgggg!" Mirah exhaled while rubbing both hands up her face.

For a long time, she replayed her dreams. Both of them involved Mr. Blondie. Who was he? Was he real or just her overworked mind trying to deal with the pilling workload she had?

⌘⌘⌘⌘⌘⌘

Across town, near the bay, another body was yanked from its slumber. But different questions swirled around in its mind. The floor to ceiling glass window providing a breathtaking view of the calm water, disturbed only by a few pleasure boots headed out to sea. The water, with all the horror it was associated with, keeps this one connected somehow to a life far behind. With a sigh, long legs reached over the bed's side for the cool, marble tiled floor. Long strides soon had toes warming with the morning's kiss as it stood before the large pane of glass. *How did she do it? No human has ever connected with me in such a way. All of her essence was intertwined with mine. I could feel her confusion, taste her humanity. Hmmm, delightful. She's close, somewhere in this city. My city; it and all its humans.*

Flyenz!

Yes, Master, a voice sounded in Ayularc's ears.

I have a job for you. There is a female human I need found; discreetly. Let none of the others know what you are doing. Keep your thoughts to yourself, understood?

Yes, Master. Of course, Master.

Good. I will share with you a taste of her humanity. When you find it, you find her. Do not approach, only watch and observe her routine for three days. I want video as well. Bring your intel directly to me no matter where I am at the time; interrupt if you must. Understood?" Ayularc repeated the word, but this time it had a threatening tone. He knew it wasn't necessary as his aid of over two centuries was faithful and true. But Ayularc needed to impress the urgency and importance. This human had the ability to reach beyond what should be. To reach back through time and space. To reach—him.

⌘⌘⌘⌘⌘⌘

An eerie hush fell upon the crowd. Ears strained to listen for any more ripples and tears through their immediate atmosphere. Low grumbling began as questions passed between the numbers.

"Silence!" The word caused all heads to look up to a boulder off in the distance. "We all felt and heard it. Still nothing, and I mean nothing, changes our course. We press ahead as planned. Everyone, contact your offspring. Find out who the breach is, the weak link. I want them brought to me at once!"

Without another comment, the crowd disbursed. Feet caused the earth to shake beneath every step. It sounds like that of static electricity echoed all around. From the vantage point of the boulder, the leader looked out before him. Concerned lines on his face turned to one forming a laugh. The laugh was boisterous, rising from the pits of his stomach, focused on the sky above.

"So you decide to try and throw a stumbling block before us? No matter. What can one human do to us? We are strong; we have an army and continue to add to the numbers. We both know nothing can stop what is to come. It is written!"

Nothing. No response came. None was expected, but the acknowledgment of the new tool being used against them was received. Even though much was written, recorded in eternity, still to be played out there in the physical realm, the stakes were still high. High enough for all involved to give everything to prove their point.

"No holds barred, as the humans say huh? Okay then, NO HOLDS BARRED!"

CHAPTER 4

The recurring issue with the formula was that human emotions' instability proved more than the hybrids could manage after extensive interaction among people. Those who were noticed to be on the verge of losing control were recalled as it were—recycled to be precise. Skin, hair, and organs were used in further experiments with DNA manipulation. *Our kind do their best to always keep a level of self-control. Human emotions gone awry means certain death to us. Whatever this is, however possible, I must figure it out, rip it out before I am tossed into an endless void again. There is no telling how long it will be before another flesh suit is made for me.*

"No!" The resonant vibration made by Ayularc's fist hitting the stone countertop almost made the crystal goblet shatter. "I will not move to the back of the line. I have not been free to roam Earth for the past 210 years, governing over cities, hundreds of thousands of souls only to be regarded as a failure, defective."

Ayularc. The voice was unmistakable.

Father.

There is little time, my son. I know you are the one through whom the human passed through the void to our realm. She is strong. I fear she is much more than you can handle. Meet me at the place of your birth, alone within the hour.

As you wish, Father, Ayularc replied, his voice never wavering to show that the much sooner than expected summoning pulled at the fine tethers of his long dominated humanity.

⌘⌘⌘⌘⌘⌘

Flyenz had been combing the city for almost a week. A needle in a haystack search it was, well, almost. He did have an advantage, though. The sample of humanity his master, Ayularc, had given was enough to set in place a detection net, if you will, to pick up any traces of it emanating from humans within the net's range. It was all based on using Fylenz's spiritual abilities. Humans who're being tracked in the net were clueless about what was going on. He had decided to start from the outskirts of the city opposite from where Ayularc's home was. He figured the human could not have been close to his master because Ayularc would have detected the human himself.

Just before Flyenz was about to move on to another area, he got a hit. It was faint, so he adjusted his detection range, and within twenty minutes, he had a location. The address was for an apartment building, corner unit, second floor. Flyenz sat in his car, parked halfway down the block from the pinged location. From where he was, he could watch all going in and out of the building. Quick foot surveillance of the area confirmed no back doors, only a fire escape on each short side of the building.

He tensed up a little when he picked up on the tracked humanity coming from a relatively short stocky woman, holding the hand of a little girl leaving the building. Only to relax when seeing it fade away after a few minutes. *She must have touched the woman recently. Humanity only lasts on surfaces for about ten minutes.* Thankful for the overcast skies, Flyenz adjusted his legs and got comfortable in the driver's seat. *This could take a while. Or maybe not.*

Mirah emerged from the building's front door, busy looking at her cell phone before holding it to her head as if listening to someone speaking. Without saying a word, she ended the call and unlocked a parked small red sedan. Flyenz waited for her to drive off before tailing her. Thirty minutes later, she arrived at a tall office building deep in the city. She'd parked in an all-day parking garage before stopping at a coffee shop drive-thru.

With the hidden lapel pin recording everything, Flyenz followed Mirah, blending in with the small group of people headed into the building. Fiddling with his cell phone, he pretended not to notice the set of office doors Mirah entered. Satisfied he was not noticed, Flyenz took a still photo with his phone of the company name plaque hanging on the wall next to the set of doors. Cityscape Daily glared back at him through the lens. A quick Internet search informed him that it was a local newspaper, considered one of the top three in the city. Further searches led Flyenz to the newspaper's website. On a page listing staff, Mirah's smile arrested his fingers. They froze for a moment, then fumbled slightly as Flyenz took a screenshot of the webpage.

He spent the rest of the day hanging out in the lobby and across the street, browsing in a few of the stores, all the while keeping his eyes peeled for any sign of Mirah. Flyenz didn't have too long of a wait as she appeared with a small group headed towards his side of the street. A look at his cell phone indicated it was approaching noon, and he suspected the group was on the hunt for lunch. Keeping his distance, he stepped onto the busy sidewalk, keeping just enough space from the group to hear some of what was being said.

"I really don't know how much longer I can keep this diet up," the woman to Mirah's left said. "I mean, it's like I'm always hungry. These small portions and food restrictions will be the death of me!"

"Come on, Paula, it's not that bad. Haven't you lost some weight already? Besides, you have a goal to get off of your medications and not to mention, turn the head of the UPS delivery guy. Don't think we don't see you flirting every day when he comes through the door."

"Oh, be quiet, Jean," Paula almost sang, blushing as she did.

"I think you're doing a great job Paula. Don't mind Jean or anyone else for that matter. Still remember, you are doing this for you. If Mr. UPS doesn't appreciate you for who you are and not what you are working towards looking like, his loss." Mirah squeezed the woman's shoulders as she spoke.

Several strides later, they were entering a small deli. The line was not too long, but if Flyenz went inside, he would have no room to hide. Instead, he walked past the deli's door and opted to grab a sandwich from a street cart three shops down the sidewalk. The women exited the deli about twenty minutes later and headed back toward their office building. Instead of going inside, they grabbed a few vacant spots of a picnic bench just north of the parking garage Mirah had parked her car. With no place to look inconspicuous, Flyenz opted to remain on the opposite side of the street. By 12:55 PM, the women hugged, and while the others went back into the office building, Mirah headed towards the parking garage. Typical of the area, a sudden rain downpour had people running for shelter. Flyenz used the opportunity to get to his car parked in an open, uncovered parking lot. He readied himself to follow Mirah the moment he saw her red sedan snake its way down the multi-leveled parking garage.

For two more days, he followed Mirah's movements. Recording any new places she visited, which were mostly food spots and twice, a church about three blocks away from her apartment building. There she met with worshipers once for choir rehearsal and another for prayer. Flyenz kept his distance both times, not because he was afraid of the church grounds, but he knew he'd easily be spotted as not being a regular. He could tell those that were in attendance on both occasions were well acquainted. *I'm here to observe and report, nothing more;* he reminded himself.

At night he easily managed to slip into Mirah's apartment building. The main entrance door required a key card, but its electric circuitry was no match for Flyenz's ability to manipulate energy. That also meant the lobby surveillance camera would glitch before and as he passed by, no evidence of him ever being there would be recorded. Considering the number of units in the building, many of the tenants once inside didn't venture out until the next morning. It meant less need for stealth by Flyenz, making him happy. By the morning of the fourth day, armed with video footage and a few souvenirs he'd taken from Mirah's apartment while she slept, Flyenz headed towards Ayularc's house. They had agreed the exchange of information only be done there.

CHAPTER 5

A week prior to Flyenz starting his tracking of Mirah, Ayularc made the trip to the mountain's cave where he was born. Well, it wasn't his original birthsite but the place his DNA was found, and he was reborn in a manner of speaking. The mountain was not too far west of the city. For him, he could make the trip within the hour timeframe his father had given. It was the reason Ayularc had settled there. The place wouldn't let him go; no matter where he traveled, he felt grounded walking on the land his original body last did. When he first returned, he set out to have the area deemed a landmark. The formation of charity fronts, keeping it a historic site, throughout the years helped keep most humans away. Ayularc didn't want the area disturbed since the search for DNA of his kind lost in The Flood continued to this day.

Ayularc stood quite short in comparison to his father. The Fallen One, now forever changed into his current form, towered over Ayularc's 6' 4" slender frame. Seeing him always made Ayularc face the reality of his existence. Not to rule, as many thought he did during his day to day operations, but to serve. Without turning to face his son, Ayularc's father spoke,

"Of all created, I never thought it would be you. You—losing control over your humanity. What sparked this, do you know?"

"No, father. I have been reflecting on events since it happened. Still, nothing stands out, yet."

"The word has been given that we are to report at once when the weak link has been made known. You are my pride, Ayularc. Of all the human women I had seeded, your birth the first to give me much pride. I know losing your beloved was—challenging, but you are Nephelim, and we were able to return your spirit to another flesh suit. Your DNA was the catalyst to the rebirth of our army. Weakness can not be found among the ranks!"

"I understand, father."

"Your tone betrays you. Something about the loss of love threatens to unravel all the years you have tightened around your humanity. Do not make me have to turn you over to him. His wrath will destroy you. Turn whatever you must into hate. Then turn hate into an unquenchable desire to survive. We must have human blood to complete our agenda," Ayularc's father said, turning to face him, head bent down to shorten the distance between their faces. With a deep sigh, he continued, “love, my son, is a powerful weapon. I was almost consumed by it at the death of your mother. I wanted offspring, yes, but I knew the cost of it for the women we seeded. Of all the human women, she—she reached me, similar to how this woman has reached you. The only thing that saved me from his wrath was the fact all of us who chose to turn against The Creator was needed to build an army. My role was not yet complete. Then I had to do the unthinkable, pledge you, the offspring who bore the most of my DNA as a loyal subject to him. It was my penance, you could say.”

Ayularc stood in silence for a moment, peering as deep as he could in his father’s eyes. Breaking the silence, he asked,

“What will I give as penance? I have no offspring to give should I not be able to undo the damage to my current existence.”

A glimmer, and only a glimmer, of sadness, ever so slightly turned down the corners of Ayularc’s father's eyes.

“You will have to give then, as a sacrifice, the thing or one you love most. Only then you may be able to stay the wrath which will return your spirit into The Void for a time.”

The cool breeze that rose off the mountain's side did little to cool down the rage building in Ayularc. He had sworn to himself never to be so overcome by his humanity since The Flood that he couldn't regain control. Never to allow the need of another to replace the need for self-preservation. But here he was, the very notion clawing at this resolve.

On the morning when Flyenz showed up at his home, he reflected again over the meeting he'd had with his father. The look in his eyes, the warning in his voice. Ayularc checked his composure when Flyenz entered the large foyer.

"As you requested, Master. I found the human after a week on the other side of the city. Mirah Drysen," Flyenz paused after the name's indication to the sex of the human, not sure what reaction if any, his master would show. Content it was safe to continue speaking, he said, "works for the Cityscape Daily. She has a column with the newspaper, which has a pretty impressive following, and a personal blog online. The online blog, though, you may find interesting. It has a lot of posts with regards to prayer and dreams."

The mention of the blog's focus did indeed get a reaction, albeit small, still a reaction nonetheless from Ayularc. Handing a bag with some personal items taken from Mirah's apartment, Flyenz went on to say, "these I collected while she was asleep." Ayularc's eyes flashed to Flyenz, not in surprise but wanting to confirm he left no trace of the intrusion. "No, Master. I left no physical evidence of my presence. Also, the items were mostly things buried under stuff around the apartment. They looked as if they hadn't been touched in a long time. Here is a thumb drive containing the videos and still shots I took while following her movements. Pretty boring life she lives, if you ask me."

"Thank you, Flyenz. You may go now and remember, no one else is to know about this. It would be unfortunate if they did," Ayularc's expression was warning enough for Flyenz. He had been with his master for over 120 years, no further explanation or interpretation was needed.

"I'll see myself out, Master. You know how to reach me if whenever my services are needed," Flyenz uttered quietly while backing up to the front door.

The heavy wooden door closed with a low pitched thud. Silence once again engulfed Ayularc. His pulse had begun to quicken as he inserted the thumb drive into his laptop. Eagerly his fingers pressed the touchpad opening the drive. He started the first of many videos. Bouncing brown curls danced around the shoulders of a petite woman. Honey highlights glistened in the sunlight. Skin colored as if dipped in maple syrup, momentarily took him back to when he and others gathered nectar for their community brimming with humans. Shaking his head, he focused on the present. For hours he sat staring at the videos Flyenz provided. Then the still photos he'd taken of her driving a small red sedan, walking along the sidewalk, gazing out of her apartment window, entering and leaving a church building.

How is she not married? Was she widowed? Certainly, there were men interested in her. Or maybe she is the one not taken by their advances. The way she carries herself, I'd say the latter.

"Mirah Drysen. Mirah," Ayularc said, dragging out her first name again at the end. "Hmmm, what's so special about you? Well, Mirah, I intend to find out and quickly."

Ayularc's father had been doing his best to throw any suspicion away from his direction, but he knew time was not going to be accommodating for long. He had to get the facts without delay. He needed to meet this, Mirah Drysen. Some things required doing in person.

With fingers dancing across the laptop's keyboard, Ayularc scanned the posts of her blog. He noticed a pattern, Mirah was using the blog as a way to send encrypted messages to a large percentage of her subscribers. The trail was easy for him to follow but may take some time for a human to notice if they weren't looking. Mirah was busy gathering information from anyone else who'd experienced dreams that were vivid, coupled with unexplainable events during waking hours. She also was compiling a list of the people who had started to go missing in and around the city for the past five years.

Further digging revealed a close friend of hers disappeared about that same time. Vanished without a trace, and the police were unable to give any closure regarding what happened. The name of the person she lost in the post's photo was tagged as Tito Manuez. *Ahh, wait, that was not just a friend; he was her husband.* A photo showed she wore a press badge with the name Mirah Drysen Manuez.

A plan formulated in Ayularc's mind. *Every mouse trap needs bait, and I have just the thing for setting a trap for Mirah.* Using Mirah's blog contact form to send an anonymous message, Ayularc told her he had information that could be useful in finding out what happened to her husband. He instructed her to meet him the next day for lunch at Cannes Café, which was about halfway between where they both lived. He provided an email account used for private business for her to confirm she'd be there. Within fifteen minutes, three words were replied, "I'll be there."

A devilish smirk reflected back to Ayularc from his laptop's screen as he stared at Mirah's reply. *Prompt, I like that.* He continued to scan through her blog posts, trying to get a feel for her personality, her likes, hobbies, anything to give him more of an advance. Satisfied, he'd gathered all he could, Ayularc shut off his laptop and went to raid his kitchen. Chef was always leaving tasty treats around, and from what he suspected, Ayularc knew he was going to be using a lot of mental and spiritual energy engaging with this woman who somehow reached cross into the spirit realm to him.

CHAPTER 6

Toying with a lock of his hair, as a finger scrolled words suspended in the air before him, the tall one asked, "What is it?"

"We've noticed an uptick in Internet activity regarding missing humans. Comments are coming in from around the world, describing some unusual early morning activities as well as poorly shot footage."

"Oh? Do you have a central location where all of this data is being filtered?"

"Somewhat. So far, we've discovered 120 IP Addresses, and that is within the United States alone."

"Really? Well, we couldn't expect them to not notice something," exhaling slowly, the tall one continued, "things were so much simpler before the rise of technology in the hands of humans."

"But Lu, we were the ones that gave them tech building blocks..."

"I'm well aware, Dracious!," smoothing the front of his vest, Lu turned and gazed at the now slightly head bent brother in arms. "All I was saying was things were less complicated. We didn't have to worry about there being accessible evidence. Yes, we needed them to become more technically inclined to fit our agenda. Still, their thirst for knowledge and relentless ambitions, we didn't properly calculate their tenaciousness, even if they were made lesser than us. Whatever spiritual shortcomings they have, they make up for it with courage and the will to survive. An animal with nothing to lose is a dangerous one; never forget that!"

"Yes, Brother."

"Any updates on who allowed the human to connect with them?"

"No, but everyone is working to discover the weak link. What do you want us to do about the 120 IP Address owners?"

"Gather them up—slowly. Have one of our Branded to replicate their devices and periodically interact with incoming messages and posts. I don't want to sound any premature alarms."

"Understood."

"What of the prototype ships? Are we on schedule for deployment?"

"Yes. We're just waiting on a few more shipments of human blood to power the circuitry. The crew members have grown to maturity and have completed their training."

"And the Humtracks?"

"New litters are being conditioned weekly. Each litter averages about 600."

"Any females yet?"

"Not yet."

Lu let out a disappointing sigh as he took five paces to his left. "No matter. If we must create them the hard way, so be it. Keep me posted on the owners of those IP Addresses. Have someone more persuasive, who possess the art of diplomacy to meet with them. I want them under the impression we have information related to their searches to trade. Give them some trails that lead nowhere. But first, get them to give us complete access, and not just to their contacts, but also their spirits."

"Consider it done."

When he was alone again, Lu turned his attention back to the words, still suspended in the air. His gaze focused beyond them over the vast landscape. Their punishment was to live on the earth but not directly interact with it. Instead, they viewed the world as if through a one-way mirror. They were able to see, but not touch—until now.

After millennia, their tests and experiments birthed means to not only make their offspring tangible again but vessels that could pierce through the mirror-like barrier. They'd mixed their DNA with that of every creature, both known and unknown to mankind until they'd created one that could track mankind's humanity. Humtracks. These creatures had the keen ability of smell, taken from dogs and agility, stealth, and reproductive capacity of spiders. Their appearance, too, had proven useful as it struck the hearts of man, paralyzing them with fear at their grotesqueness.

By his calculations, Lu estimated they would soon be able to begin phase two of the plan. The seasonal storms were starting to increase in many parts of Earth, and things were already in place to create the desired level of panic among people. Those in power had been informed that it was time to put on the performance of their lives. All of their family's wealth and prestige had come with a price tag many thought had been forgotten since generations in their bloodline had died out. How foolish they'd become. Did they not read the fine print, albeit was extremely fine and somewhat faded due to much time passing since initially signed. Still, a deal is a deal, and these covenants have no expiration dates.

⌘⌘⌘⌘⌘⌘

Mirah rechecked her reflection in her car's rearview mirror. With a deep breath, she stared back at herself. With hands gripping the steering wheel, she gave herself a pep talk.

"Alright, if this person has information about Tito, it'll be worth coming alone. Besides, this is a public place, and no one would dare try anything in broad daylight. Well, mostly daylight. What is up with these storm clouds lately? I know we are in the season for them, but, geessh. All these clouds do is hover without one drop of rain already. Ahh, it could be worse though; the clouds have made it cooler, much cooler."

With slightly shaking hands, Mirah gathered her handbag and got out of the car. She'd parked a ways down the block from the café, hoping to take in any out of place people or vehicles. Nothing. The street was busy with pedestrians and cars. Everyone was doing their own thing, none paying any particular interest to her. She'd chosen to wear her comfortable pair of black ankle boots. They made her stride with more confidence than she really had, especially now. A small smile crossed her face as a slight breeze filled the space between her torso and loose-fitting blouse, lifting into the air notes of sugared berries and warmed vanilla from Mirah's favorite body cream. The wide knee-length skirt danced around her legs from the combination of breeze and bounce in her walk.

This is for Tito, she told herself. *Must find out what happened to him. There is no way he just took off. Granted, we'd been having some issues in our marriage, but we were starting to turn things around. No way he just—left me. No way!* Mirah collected herself as she stepped into the entrance of the café. She pushed back thoughts of doubt and hurt, squared her shoulders, and with chin raised, entered the café.

The delectable aromas of coffee and fresh-baked treats made Mirah's stomach come alive. Thankful for the background music of whimsical orchestra, she smiled as a waiter greeted her.

"Welcome to Cannes Café. How many are in your party?"

"Thank you. Ahh, I'm meeting someone. I was told to just provide my name; Mirah Drysen."

"Mirah Drysen," the young man said, dragging out her last name as his index finger moved down a piece of paper on the small podium. "Here you are, Mirah Drysen," he said, confirming her name was on the list. "Great, right this way, please. Your party is already here."

Mirah followed the man through the café as he snaked through several already occupied tables. The sound of mixed conversations, interrupted by the occasional coffee cup clanging to sources, made a mix match yet still beautiful accompaniment to the music piped through strategically placed ceiling speakers. Trying not to smack the heads of anyone seated, Mirah grabbed her handbag, putting it to her chest. When she noticed the waiter's feet had stopped moving, she abruptly halted, head raising, eager to discover who her mystery lunch date was.

An inclined head and deep eyes met her shocked expression of recognition. Mouth now freakishly dry, Mirah feared she would faint. The room seemed to start sliding to her right. Movement around her blurred along with voices, as pressure and support of a powerful arm circled her waist—then the remnants of daylight became like night.

The rim of a chilled glass rested against her lips. Cool water kissed them, wanting to get in. Then a voice. It sounded strange in a sense; it wasn't like any tone of voice Mirah had heard before. It sounded almost like several voices speaking in unison.

"Here, drink. You're okay, just a little lightheaded. Have you eaten anything at all so far today?"

"Umm, what? Umm, no, actually I woke up late and was rushing to get here; missed breakfast."

"I see. Open. Eat this piece of croissant. I took the liberty of ordering you a bowl of vegetable soup for starters."

Embarrassed and stretching her eyes wide in attempts to make them focus, Mirah's eyes first landed on the bowl of seeming soup before her. The glass of water now placed next to it, and the body of the voice seated opposite on the other side of the small table. *I don't remember seeing him move away. Were my eyes closed that long. Oh, God, how crazy I must look, fainting and all, but I'm not sure hunger caused my reaction.*

Tension swirled around them. The sounds of the café blotted out, even though people were talking and eating. Silence, all but for the beating of her heart.

"You can relax, no need to be apprehensive, afraid. We are here to exchange information as it were."

"I know you," Mirah choked out. Saliva production had started again. She reached for the glass of water and downed half of the cool liquid. With a slight trembling of her hand, she placed it back on the table.

"Yes, you can say we know each other, but only superficially. I'd like to remedy that."

"I'm supposed to be meeting someone who has information about Tito Maurez. Just what information can *you* possibly give me about him?"

"Nothing."

Mirah's cheeks became flushed, and her eyes flashed an angry stare. "You're telling me you lured me here under false pretense? Aww, that was low to use someone close to me for whatever sick game you're playing! Tito could be hurt, in trouble or..." Mirah paused, not wanting to say the words that taunted her.

"I apologize for any additional harm my ruse has caused, but I can assure you, I'm playing no game here. The stakes are quite high."

Mirah sat there for a moment until the aroma of the soup could no longer be ignored. As polite as possible, she took the soup spoon and ate. Eerie silence again shielded them from everyone nearby. She did her best to pretend she didn't notice. The hairs on the back of her neck and arms reacted by rising, and it wasn't from the heat of the soup she swallowed.

Satisfied that she'd had enough food in her stomach to keep her upright, he placed both of his elbows on the table, fingers laced under his chin.

"Your name is Mirah Drysen Manuez. Married Tito Manuez almost twelve years ago. His disappearance caused you to shift your blog's post content from purely inspirational to targeting a, shall we call them, special group of thinkers. Your faith is strong. You have an active prayer life, and if not every night, then almost, you have vivid, sometimes unexplainable dreams. Not too long ago, you had one that seemed wiped from your memory when you awoke. But from the look in your eyes, it's all starting to come back."

"How do you know all of this? Granted, some is easy enough to find out with social media and all, but how do you know about my dreams, specifically?" Mirah managed to get the words out in one breath, afraid this too was another vivid dream. She wasn't about to let it end if it were. She needed answers.

"I know about your dreams, specifically, because we shared one. The one you couldn't lately recall until you saw my face." He waited intentionally for a few moments so that her brain could catch up to what was happening, what had already happened. "My name is Ayularc."

Mirah gasped was louder than even Ayularc expected. He thought her eyes could get no bigger than what they had been when she first saw him sitting at the table before fainting; he was wrong.

"MR. BLONDIE?!"

Hmmm, new name, I think. I've been called by so many through the ages but not too original, Ayularc thought, studying Mirah's death gaze. *I swear, if she doesn't stop having these moments of not breathing, I won't be able to get the information I need from her. Well, at least audibly; I suppose I could reach her mind, but that could hasten my inevitable discovery. Someone else will have to take my place in all of this. No way I'm going to be expelled from this flesh suit. I've got a lot of things left to do and of all I've had to wear, this one fits my personality most so far. Mr. Blondie huh? I wonder what else about me took hold of her memories, as did my hair color, which obviously struck a chord?*

CHAPTER 7

Rows of craft, nearly silent, hovered a foot off the ground. Humtracks were being loaded. From a distance, they looked like single file large black army ants. Following alongside were failed regeneration experiments. Those that had a fair to adequate range of body movement were kept alive. Their one purpose was to obey the orders of The Fallen, commanders of every mission through mind links. Once through the barrier, they followed the instructions of The Fallen's offspring.

Each ship was being deployed to a designated city in a few countries. This would be a test run before unfolding everything on the earth. There were stockpiles of blood awaiting transport and new humans to be turned into volunteers, based on their Rh-negative blood type. Lu strode through the purposeful flow of activity. Pride filled his chest as he envisioned the unfolding of his plans.

"Soon, we will be adding to our ranks by the hour. With the influx of fresh human blood, our crafts will be innumerable in the sky. Not to mention the amount of DNA to supply the flesh suits still needed that the wandering offspring require. But it's the discarded bodies of the volunteers that excite me the most. With them, we'll have everything we need to bring back the giants—our pride and marvelous creations. We will rule this world again; it is written," Lu hissed under his breath while his face displayed a calm smile, eyebrows raising as he nodded to those who passed by.

⌘⌘⌘⌘⌘⌘

"Wait, you're telling me what I thought was a forgotten dream was not actually one? And that you are a..." Mirah blinked hard, taking in the man, or whatever he was sitting across the small table from her. "You're a Neph," she inhaled deeply, trying to calm herself and lower her rising voice, "you're a Nephilim? As in the men of renown in the Bible?"

"Yes," Ayularc replied calmly, eyes fixed on her looking for any signs she might faint again. She didn't, but most of her coloring did fade away momentarily.

"Shhhh, I've known that a lot of what's happened to me wasn't random, but I never guessed I'd be singled out, so to speak. Everything in the dream was real? It all happened?"

"The part with being in the mouth of the mountain cave, the water everywhere, that body which was not yours, yes, that happened—to me over three thousand years ago. The other parts of your dream are events to come. What you described seeing, those plans you can say, have not unfolded yet." Ayularc signed, he had no understanding why he divulged such secret information. He shifted for the first time since sitting down in the chair after she had regained consciousness. He was uneasy around her.

"What does this all mean?" The plea sprung from Mirah's lips; questioning eyes searched his.

"It means there is little time—for you."

"Me? Why do you say that?" Panic returned to her, the little control she'd managed nearly shattered.

"It means that you have become a target. No human was to have any insight into what is taking place beyond the barrier." He paused, seeing her eyes question what the barrier was. "The barrier is what many would describe as the veil between the physical and spiritual worlds. I need to figure out how you were able to cross it and why I was the one you reached when you did."

"Does this mean you're running out of time too? Is there a target on your back?"

"Running out of time, maybe. If I don't figure things out, having a target on my back will be a trivial matter compared to what my immediate future would hold."

"Your kind can't die as we do, can they? I mean, The Word says you don't have a soul to redeem."

"True, but our existence when death occurs to our body is an indescribable torment. One I'd rather not be forced back to so quickly."

"Forced back to, as in you were able to leave death?"

"Yes. This body you see has been my flesh..., *my body* for only 47 years. I've been living on the earth for about 210 years already."

Furrowed eyebrows and a curious stare moved across Ayularc, starting from his hair down to the slender fingers of his hands. He saw Mirah take in his height, though that of many human men, based on the amazement reflection of her pupils, he may as well have been the height of the body her spirit had reached. Her gaze unsettled him. He sat there, disturbingly still, like a living statue. After Mirah's third attempt to speak, he broke the silence,

"How?" He asked, a sheepish smile tugging at his face.

“Yes. I mean you are, sorry, your spirit is old,” she slowly started before finishing with a rush of words and building excitement, “yet here you are, in a body that for all pretense and purposes, looks—human. How did...”

“We have learned over many, many of a human’s lifetime, how to generate these bodies. After they have been, ahh prepared, our spirits are bound to them. One benefit is that we’ve found a way to slow down the body's aging process, which allows us to enjoy them much longer had we not.”

“Generate? Prepare? Do I even want to know what bonding means?”

With curiosity, he looked at her, now over the rim of a glass of water, which did little to remedy the dryness near the back of his throat. *Why does she unsettle me so? I have to get to the bottom of this, this, whatever THIS IS! No telling how much time there is before I’m discovered.* Focusing on keeping his voice as emotionless as possible, Ayularc gently placed the glass on the linen-covered table, surprising himself he was about to share with a human secrets none other who knew remained alive to tell.

“Generated is a term we use to describe the process of when human DNA is mixed with ours to ahhh, clone if you would, a humanoid body for the wandering Nephilim spirits to inhabit. Similar to how your body wears clothes, our spirits wear these flesh suits. The bodies are prepared as soulless shells, to full adult size in about 13 months. They are kept in something like an incubator, which is constructed from remains of the unwanted and forgotten. The bonding occurs when our spirits are summoned by our fathers."

Mirah sat in her chair; this time, she was the one imitating a living statue. The Spirit of God had whispered to her she was safe, that everything happening was planned and that she had no reason to show fear. She heeded The Spirit's voice, all but her hands, which were hidden from Ayularc's view in her lap, wringing a table napkin. She didn't faint again, for which she was grateful. Mirah barely blinked because she wanted to burn to memory every detail of this moment, of him. The longer she sat there, the more of her first dream she recalled. Without warning, her voice erupted,

"I'm sure I don't want to know what you mean by the construction of the incubators, but I must. Since you are sharing this information with me, no doubt you want something in exchange. I may as well know just what I'm being set up for." No longer was a wide-eyed woman seated across from him, but one who had found her voice, her courage, her spiritual authority.

Ayularc smiled openly, liking this newfound confidence in Mirah. He inclined his head a little, then leaned back in his chair.

"As you wish. We collect humans who have fallen victim to crimes, untimely deaths, and when those supply channels run dry, we collect run-a-ways, those living on the streets, the forgotten and unseen by others. We separate blood, flesh, and bone, repurposing each to make the rather large required incubators..."

"You mean wombs," Mirah interjected.

"Yes, the rather large wombs needed to generate..."

"Say it for what it is. You mean grow."

"Very well. I will speak plainly to you since you prefer the direct approach."

Mirah flashed a fake smile.

Ayularc continued, "The wombs are filled with the collected blood, and both human and our DNA are mixed together, creating a new DNA strand. Cells form, and then they are placed in the wombs to—grow." He caught Mirah's head tilt as if to say he'd left out a part. Objecting to her unspoken statement, he added, "the flesh collected is used to construct the wombs, heat is applied to fuse the pieces together."

"This summoning you speak of, is this how your spirit crossed the barrier from the place you went when you died?"

"Yes."

"And you can travel between the physical and spiritual realms?"

"Yes, due to the fact we have the DNA of our fathers and that of human mothers, we can exist in both realms."

"So what does that say about me then? I'm human, and somehow, I was able to cross the barrier."

"Yes, you did," Ayularc confirmed, squinting his eyes slightly as if trying to look even deeper into her soul. As if searching for a hidden clue, "but only your spirit, not your physical body."

The waiter's arrival at the table with a pitcher of iced water broke the tension swirling around them. He cleared his throat before asking if either of them cared for more water. Ayularc shook his head, indicating they didn't while asking for the check without breaking the staring match he and Mirah were locked in. Hurriedly the waiter left.

"Wait, I still have a lot of questions to ask you? I'm nowhere done," Mirah all but demanded.

"You have fight, I'll give you that. No doubt that has something to do with how you were able to cross the barrier. Don't lose it; you're going to need every ounce, soon. This is not the best place to continue our discussion. If you want, we can go somewhere more quiet with fewer eyes on us."

Mirah thought for a moment at Ayularc's suggestion. The waiter returned with a check. Without even looking to see what was owed, Ayularc gave the man a crisp hundred dollar note instructing him to keep that change. Happily nodding, the man thanked him for the generous tip, inviting them to come back anytime.

"Where is this quiet place you have in mind?"

"May I hold your cell phone?" Ayularc asked, extending the long fingers of his left hand. His fingertips brushed Mirah's as she handed the device to him. The painful burn of their contact seemed only to affect him. He played off the incident as if it never occurred. However, Mirah caught the ever so slight wince pulling at his eyes.

What was that? Why did he wince when our fingers touched? Was that your doing Father? A quiet voice spoke to her in that instant, assuring her that it was her faith and belief which allowed the Fire of Heaven to keep a constant hedge of protection around her.

Moments later, Ayularc slid Mirah's cell phone across the small space of the table's surface. He gave her a strained smile then said,

"I've placed my contact information and home address in it. So it's easy for you to find, I listed it under Mr. Blondie. Are you free for dinner tonight? You needn't worry; you are well protected. I can not harm you as long as the fire encircles your body." Mirah looked at him, surprised, wondering if he could hear her thoughts, her conversation with God. "I can feel it," Ayularc finished seeing questions behind her eyes.

"Sure, why not. You've already given me enough of a warning that I'm running out of time, and I have to know why."

"Around 7:00 PM?" Ayularc asked, standing, helping Mirah with her chair.

"I'll see you at 7:00 PM," Mirah said, adjusting her clothes as they started to exit the café.

The sound of thunder alerted them that another downpour was fast approaching. Without thinking much, Mirah waved and dashed towards her parked car. When she was sitting in the driver's seat again, she let the music from the speakers hug her while she waited for an opening in the traffic to pull away from the curb.

"WHAT JUST HAPPENED?" She screamed to no one. Holding her chest, now being bombarded with heavy beats of her heart, she repeated the question above a whisper, "what just happened?"

CHAPTER 8

The exterior of the house was of straight lines and flat walls. The occasional long, narrow window broke the surface of slate-colored concrete. *It fits him*, Mirah thought as she steadied her breathing before exiting her car. Salty air tickled her nose as gentle waves splashed against nearby barrier walls. Soft yellow lighting lined the stone path, leading to the dark wood-stained oversized front door. Motion sensor lights suddenly illuminated the last fifty feet, and seconds later, the front door slowly opened—perfectly timed.

Before Mirah could break her stride, Ayularc motioned for her to continue into the house with a wave of his arm.

"So glad you came," he said with a smile that initially didn't match his eyes until he caught Mirah's lingering stare, quickly adjusting his expression.

Mirah walked into the open space, quickly trying to take in everything as she stepped further into the space. Save for a large sectional, an oversized side chair, and a thick shaggy rug; the living area was sparsely furnished. Several odd-shaped art pieces hung on the walls. The night's gentle breeze again greeted her, this time through two sets of glass floor-to-ceiling open windows. The sound of the water from the bay was hypnotic.

"Do have a seat. Would you care for something to drink? Dinner is almost ready."

"Ahh, water would be nice, thanks."

"Ice?"

"No, thank you," Mirah replied, eyes transfixed on the bay, following a wave before it merged into another. Seeing the body of water so close left her feeling unusually unsettled. She quickly shook her head and shoulders, playing with a tourmaline stone set in a gold band ring, before turning her attention to one of the pieces of art on a nearby wall. Her reaction to the water didn't go unnoticed by Ayularc.

Before Mirah could miss his absence, Ayularc returned with a tall glass of water. He managed to hand it to Mirah without their fingers touching, the unpleasantness of which he was currently not in the mood to experience. The memory of the pain he'd experienced earlier was still fresh.

"Interesting pieces you have. Not quite sure what it's meant to be?" Mirah said with her head tilted to the left as if that angle would provide some hints as to what she'd be staring at.

"They are based on a painting from another lifetime."

"You paint?"

"I used to, but that is a pleasure given up due to the loss of my muse."

"I see," Mirah said softly, sensing the sadness behind the smile Ayularc's face still wore. Wanting to lighten the mood, she continued, "why this house? I mean, the view is breathtaking and doesn't sound like you have many neighbors to worry about regarding noise."

"Yes, well proximity to the bay was a key factor, and indeed, privacy is important. I purchased the surrounding three acres of land and had the house custom built."

"I'm sure you had, or should I say, have your reasons for privacy and the custom build," Mirah said with a smile and a raised eyebrow.

"Dinner's ready. Right this way," Ayularc said, arm stretched toward a hallway leading off the side of the room.

I didn't hear a timer go off, nor did I notice anyone else appear in the room—wait, does he have spirits as his butler and cook? Mirah's face of concern made Ayularc quickly provide an explanation.

"I was informed when I got your glass of water the table would be ready for us within three minutes. You'll find I have a thing for punctuality." Ayularc led Mirah around the wall she'd been admiring the art piece hanging on. Against its opposite side was a relatively wide iron staircase that cut through the ceiling above. At the top of the stairs, holding onto the rail for balance, standing on the landing, Mirah gasped, pleasantly surprised to see the beautiful expanse of the bay, along with a part of the city's skyline off in the distance. A minimal amount of concrete walls obstructed the view in front of her.

"Wow!"

"Yes, it is a sight, isn't it? I had this space designed so that the glass doors rolled into the sidewalls, like pocket doors. It's often the place I come to reflect."

"Oh, I could do a lot of reflecting up here, not to mention writing. This view, wow, just wow!"

Ayularc felt amused at Mirah's excitement. He had no idea such a simple thing like a breathtaking view could change her mood so quickly. *She would have loved to see this place in its former natural glory. She would have...STOP IT! She is here to collect information from not become one of your human pets. GET A GRIP!* Ayularcs mind screamed. It was the remnants of his father's blood that always checked his human side whenever it began to become—emotional, overflowing in humanity.

Mirah was so busy staring at the view she hadn't noticed the set table to her left nor the person waiting at attention to serve them.

"Come, sit. We don't want to let the food get cold," Ayularc said now in a more demanding tone while holding the back of a chair for her to sit on.

The change in his voice caused Mirah's back to stiffen as she took the seat. She rested her small handbag on the table next to a spread of way too much food for the two of them. In front of her were an array of dishes, oddly all of which she loved most. *Strange, good, but strange,* she thought.

"I took the liberty in finding out your favorite foods. It tickles me as to how easy it is to get information on humans today. Everyone is on the Internet posting pictures of their lives. You, though, do more posts about food," he ended with a genuine smile.

"Well, writing takes a lot of energy, and I have little time to cook, so delivery and take-out on the way home are the saviors of my stomach and brain." Mirah felt unsure of how to read his mood. One minute Ayularc acted friendly, the next, intense, and just when she had braced herself for worse, he was inviting again.

"So which is it, you can cook but don't have time, or you can't cook but love to eat?"

Mirah gave him a playful smirk, "I can cook, thank you very much. I just don't have the time."

"Ah, I see," Ayularc said with an expression letting her know he didn't believe her.

They both paused, staring at each other. The reality of him being a Nephilim and she a human hit fast and hard. Sensing the change in the atmosphere, Ayularc added,

"Listen, you are safe with me. I won't hurt you. I just need to understand how you and I became connected if you will, alright?"

Mirah nodded her head slowly, a cautious smile lingering at her mouth, taking a deep breath, allowing her shoulders to relax. The scent of the delicious looking spread made her focus on a more urgent need, food. As her eyes scanned the platters, the man who was standing just a few feet away began to add a little of everything to her plate. Once they were both served, he quickly descended the staircase, and they were left alone. The sounds of the night played a wonderful tune as they sat eating in silence for several moments.

Seeing Mirah had relaxed and was satisfying the rumbling of her stomach, Ayularc decided to begin his probing gently. He noticed some of her mannerisms seemed familiar. The way she toyed with her food before gathering it on her fork. How when she was chewing, she'd momentarily close her eyes, savoring all that the mouthful surrendered. For a moment, his thoughts drifted to a distant memory. *What are the chances two could be so similar—Hmmm none at all,* he told himself.

"I hope everything is to your liking? I made sure the chef took extra care while preparing this spread."

"Umm, it's all quite delicious. Better than some I've had from anywhere," Mirah managed to get out between chews. "I appreciate the trouble, but you really didn't have to."

"From where I'm sitting, it was all worth it," Ayularc smiled, sipping a glass of water.

Mirah had noticed his beverage of choice and wondered if he drank alcohol.

"Ask your questions. I will do my best to answer—truthfully," Ayularc said softly as if he didn't want anyone else to hear, though visually they were alone.

"Oh, nothing important, I guess. I just wondered if you drank alcohol. I'm sure you indulged in a lot of wine back in the days. It was just a thought; no need bother answering it."

"Nonsense, every thought is spurred by observation and to answer your question, no and yes. No, I don't indulge in alcohol since taking this type of form. Too much will prematurely age me. Yes, in my original life, you can say I drank wine daily since it had little effect on my body." Ayularc's right cheek dimpled as he continued, "I take it you're not a big drinker?"

"I see. Ahh, no, I'm not. I've seen the stuff make people do unforgettable things. I like to have all my wits about me."

"May I ask you a question?"

"Sure," Mirah said, picking at a slice of roast beef and roasted potato on the dinner plate in front of her.

"When was your earliest dream? Wait, let me rephrase. When would you say you started to have dreams that proved to have happened or manifested some time later?"

"Hmmm," Mirah smiled, her eyes suddenly staring at nothing in particular while her mind sifted through data, locating something in particular. "I was twelve years old. I remember because for my birthday that year, an aunt had given me a small starter chemistry set. I became fascinated with nature, liquids, and metals. I'd also managed to burn a good-sized hole in my nightgown experimenting one evening in my room. Well, my parents weren't happy, to say the least, when they found me passed out from the fumes my mixture had released. The next thing I remember was waking up in a sun-filled room. I had no idea of how my clothes had been changed or how I'd ended up under the covers in bed. But I remember being somewhere unfamiliar. It wasn't until I'd sat down to have breakfast that my mom explained what happened."

Ayularc's ears perked up when he heard Mirah mention the chemistry set and passing out from some mixture's fumes. He'd seen many fall victim to something similar. Many indeed, both Nephilim and human alike. "Please, continue," he urged Mirah, who wasn't sure if he'd believe her recounting or not.

"Well, my mom said I'd been restless throughout the night. I had tossed and turned, and there were times when I was talking in my sleep, but she couldn't make out the words." Ayularc leaned in closer as Mirah continued to speak. "The words didn't make sense to her, and she thought they were a foreign language because nothing sounded like English. All she could make out and remember was, *na elle, tata yah nye*. She said I would repeat this ever so often. It wasn't until the night of my thirteenth birthday did I recall or revisit that night—in another dream.

This time, I watched myself play with the chemistry set, and some of the mixture burn a hole in my nightgown. A few seconds later, I watched my body go limp and then pass out on the floor of my bedroom. It was sometime before my mom came to check on me to say goodnight. When she found me, she became panicked and called my dad and aunt, who rushed in. It was my aunt who instructed her to quickly bathe me to remove any of the chemicals from my skin. She's a chemist and said the mixture just knocked me out, but I would be okay. Then the dream switched, and I was seeing what my younger self had seen while restless into the night.

There was a stone table, and I was lying on top of it, fully awake. I could hear a voice speaking to me from the shadows of the room," Mirah's body shivered a little as she recalled the dream. "It wanted something from me. I was refusing and starting to cry because I just wanted to go home. The voice promised I would go home right after I agreed to do what it asked."

"What did it want you to agree to?" Ayularc questioned, his eyebrows narrowing, eyes trying to connect to Mirah's distant stare.

"The voice wanted me to surrender."

"Surrender? Surrender what, exactly?"

"Surrender my will. I didn't know for sure what that meant, and so I told it that, but it only got angry and yelled it louder, SURRENDER! By this time, I was taking in deep panicked breaths and screamed, okay, just to get it over with; anything to get out of there. I pleaded to go home; I just wanted to go home."

"Then what happened?"

"I saw my body go from hysterical on the table to one almost deathly still. After a short time, I saw my mouth move, but the voice was not mine."

"What did your younger self say while on the table," Ayularc questioned, this time with his hands as tight fists under the dining table.

"Yu Elle, almost free!"

A noticeable gasp escaped Ayularc's tight lips. *Yu Elle*, he thought he would never hear those words again. *How can this be? And, na elle, tata yah nye, what does this human know of such phrases. She should have no knowledge of them since they were part of the Nephilim bonding ceremony he and all others use to bind their spirits to their new flesh suits. Mirah's playing around with chemicals was the catalyst to getting her into a deep sleep state, and no other Nephilim besides himself for miles around were more versed in alchemy than Basielle—his dead, long lost wife!*

Snapping out of her gaze, Mirah reached for a glass of water, nearly emptying it before she returned her attention to Ayularc. The liquid had managed to settle her a little. Its coolness reaffirming she was awake and in the present. She didn't think Ayularc's complexion could get any paler, but it had after listening to her. His eyes now appeared nearly black; the yellowish-gold surrounding his irises glowed brightly. He was staring intently at her; no, he was studying her, but for what?

"Did I say something wrong? The way you're looking at me, I should say, is not very comforting."

With an extended-release of his breath, Ayularc forced a smile to set Mirah at ease. His mind, however, raced with questions; his humanity bubbled over, threatening to consume him. He was acutely aware now that Mirah was more than just another human female. Somehow she had become a conduit, one connected to a very powerful and dangerous Nephilim spirit. Clearing his throat, he removed the dinner napkin from his lap and placed it on the table. His appetite was gone, or more like snatched away. Doing his best to contain countless hours of torment over the loss of his wife, Ayularc managed in as calm a voice as possible,

"No, you didn't. Actually, you shared some very interesting points that would explain how it is you were able to, shall we say, enter into my memories while you slept. Please, continue eating. Do excuse me for a few minutes though; I shall be right back." Ayularc didn't wait for Mirah's response as he made his way in an almost fluid motion to the staircase, descending before Mirah could get the first syllable out.

"Sure thing..." she said, wondering which parts, exactly, had struck this giant of a man, Nephilim, with such ferocity to his core.

CHAPTER 9

She must have figured out a way. Basielle was never a good sport at losing anything. The life she had before the waters destroyed the earth was definitely one she had planned to hold onto for a very long time. Flashes of the water's current snatching her away from the cave and him forever didn't help the emotions Ayularc was fighting to control stay at bay. Her kiss and smile, the scent of her hair, all taunted him as the realization that his wife or remnants of her were coursing their way through the body of the woman upstairs.

Focus and get a grip! Something obviously didn't go as Basielle planned because Mirah was, for the most part, in control of her body and not Basielle. It seems when Mirah is asleep when her subconscious mind is active, only then can Basielle have a measure of control. The best thing to do is question Mirah to see just how much she remembers from her dreams and if, during her woke moments, she experiences lost time or unexplained memories.

Should I tell my father what I've discovered? Hmmm, best I get more information and formulate a strategy of when I have to tell Lu that I'm the weak link. But if Basielle found a way to connect with Mirah, there may still be a chance that The Fathers can help her—all of her.

Ayularc remained motionless for a few minutes longer, staring out of the massive wall of windows onto the bay. His mind was running through several scenarios of how best to make his next move. It was near pointless to try and strategize against Lu; he was a mastermind like none other. But Ayularc had many occasions to learn from some of the best. Nephilim children grow quickly and have heightened senses shortly after birth. During the years he trained under the ever-watchful eye of his father, Ayularc had gleaned everything from the other Fathers who tutored in him all the things he'd need to know to survive Earth, his forever home.

Yes, that's it! I will help Basielle live again. She went through all of this trouble to merge with a human outside of Lu and our Fathers' approval, something I'm sure they will want to be made aware of. Her desperation, no doubt, caused the sloppy union which has left her operating as a shell of her former self. To regain Basielle her former glory, would be a great victory for our kind and, for certain, gain me the grace I'll need with Lu to be pardoned the agony of separating from this flesh suit. "Yes, I will help you, my beloved, but in return, you will owe me a debt I intend to collect," Ayularc said softly, as if not wanting anyone else to hear, then he made his way back towards the staircase.

Mirah was leaning back in her chair, water glass in hand, as she finished chewing her food. She quickly washed the remnants down with the cool liquid, dabbing the corners of her mouth with her dinner napkin before flashing Ayularc a half warm smile. Ayularc thought she was taking being in his presence pretty well. No signs of fainting, and her hands didn't shake nearly as much as he'd imagined they would. *Ahh, but I'm sure she's been praying inwardly since she arrived, and I have no plans to test my assumptions by coming into physical contact with her either. The fire in her eyes confirms all I need to know.*

"Full?"

"Quite, thanks. How about yourself, you haven't eaten much, or don't you eat—cooked food that is?"

Ayularc let out a laugh. It was no longer something he did much of, but it felt good. As spiritually frightening as she was, Mirah somehow liberated him. Probably because she had no idea how hard Nephilim try to control their humanity, something she lets freely control her. She had no idea of the rules that governed his world, no measuring stick to know when he was out of character. She was intoxicating, and he was sure that Basielle realized this too.

"I am satisfied for now, and yes, I do eat food, cooked and otherwise. Come, there is much we need to discuss, even though I find delight in watching the many facial expressions of pleasure you have while eating, that was not the reason I invited you here tonight."

"Yes, let's get to the *how* and *why* our paths have crossed at all," Mirah replied, her tone edged with seriousness, as she collected her bag and headed toward the staircase; Ayularc stood just to the side of her path, arm extended indicating he would follow her descent.

With each footstep muffled on the padding covering the metal stairs, the reality that this was not some casual dinner date caused Mirah to brace for whatever came next. She knew enough about spiritual matters to understand her dreams and reality had merged like red ink in a warm glass of milk—her life never to be as it once was. *But has it always been intertwined, and I'm just now realizing it?* She wondered, trying to disguise her wincing from the thought's gut-punch reaction, clutching her handbag to her stomach.

Opting for the side chair, Mirah did her best to appear calm. She didn't want Ayularc to notice the gravity of all that has been revealed to her lately, how it was pulling at the frayed edges of her resolve.

Sensing her rising discomfort, Ayularc allowed the plush leather of the sectional to envelop his long frame. With a touch of a nearby remote control, soft music cut through the silence. With each change in the rift, Mirah began to relax. Eventually, she accepted the support of the chairs back for her upper body. Once her heartbeat had gained a healthier rhythm, Ayularc started to what he hoped to be confirmation about theories clashing in his mind.

"Tell me, Mirah," he began, keeping his tone even and friendly, "what are some of the things you like. I mean other than food. That I have a pretty good understanding of. Tell me of the scents and colors you like. Things that fascinate you," he briefly paused, staring at her almost hypnotically, "and please don't leave out anything you may think as odd or bizarre."

The music had done a great job relaxing Mirah because, at that point, she felt like malleable clay ready to be molded. If she hadn't known better, she'd think she was drugged, but she sensed no danger in her spirit since arriving. Despite the obvious, she wasn't threatened by him. On the contrary, she found him interesting. Interesting, no; she found Ayularc, his very existence—fascinating. There were no drugs in the food she ate or the water she drank. To Mirah, Ayularc was the drug.

"Hmmm, well, I like green scents, those of leaves, trees, mints. Along with fruits and spices. I'm not one for flowery scents, like roses and chrysanthemums. Hmmm and hints of musk, yes, those are the scents I like. Ahh, as for colors, I like earth tones more, with the occasional cool color here and there. Does that help your curiosity?"

"It does, but tell me, what type of child were you? Were you friendly, shy, rambunctious?"

"I'd say friendly but more on the shy side. I mean, I had friends, but my family moved around a lot, so I found ways to play alone. Even before I understood what science was, I'd be mixing and experimenting with whatever I could get my hands on," Mirah's eyes had now drifted up the wall behind where Ayularc sat, recalling memories. "Once after the incident with the chemistry set, I did more safer experiments and discovered a love of perfumes and scented lotions. Well, it was just some baby lotion remnants and whatever pretty smelling things I could find in and around the house." A small smile pulled at her cheeks.

"Interesting." Ayularc leaned forward a little, taking in even the slightest of Mirah's movements and expressions. He missed nothing.

"Yes. I came up with my own signature blend if you will. I'd been playing outside and roaming the neighborhood for items to add to my science box. Well, that's what I called an old tin lunch box from kindergarten school. In it, I kept interesting things to take apart or add to whatever *invention* I'd be working on at the time. Anyway, I found some lavender and thought it was so pretty. When I got home, I took a few leaves of mint from my mom's herb garden. Something prompted me to get some honey from the kitchen and half of a lime I'd found in the refrigerator. Once back in my room, I crushed the lavender and mint leaves, added some honey and lime juice. I remember yelping when the lime juice got into a cut on my right hand, courtesy of my earlier foraging. I dabbed that concoction all over the house. Needless to say, my mother, in particular, wasn't so pleased with my new favorite scent. Sadly the mixture was tossed, and my parents *encouraged* me to explore other interests besides that of chemistry."

Mirah's face glowed as her eyes stared back at Ayularc, but it wasn't him she was seeing. He could tell she was reliving the memories. Just before she snapped from deep in thought, he felt for a long moment, something familiar staring back at him. A slight pull of Mirah's right cheek muscle revealed a smirk, dancing at the corner of her mouth.

"Do you miss eating honey from the honeycombs in the western garden? When the sun was high in the sky?" Ayularc chose the memory with purpose. He wanted to put a suspicion to rest or validate it. His questions were spoken softly, just enough for Mirah to hear, but soft enough to help Mirah stay in her memories trance.

“Hmmm, yes! Nothing tastes sweeter. Our bees produced the best honey in the land.”

Basielle! Ayularc didn’t know whether to feel excitement or dread. He’d need more evidence. He had to be certain. Such a thing was forbidden, except if there were spiritual, legal rights to bond with a human. But that knowledge Basielle should not know, as it was only discovered after The Flood. Ayularc looked at Mirah and wondered how her bloodline had become entangled with the trickery; blood covenant with his kind.

The fluttering wings of a seagull perching in the railing just outside the space drew Mirah’s attention back to the present. She felt a little out of sorts and shyly tugged a lock of hair behind her ear.

“Sorry, what was I saying? I was so caught up in my thoughts.”

“Oh, no worries. You had me right there with you. It sounds like you had a fun childhood.” Ayularc paused, wanting Mirah to be fully in the present. “So, did you also have honeycombs near where you lived growing up?”

“Honeycombs? Ahh no, not that I know of, at least. Besides, we only lived in the suburbs for a few years then moved closer to the city. My father had gotten some fancy job, and the commute had become too much. I spent the time up until going away to college, living in a high rise apartment building. The views were spectacular, and we even had access to a nice rooftop. Sadly though, my only interaction with nature and plants was the occasional visit to the city's central park." Mirah, paused looking at Ayularc with a puzzled expression, "so why'd you ask me about honeycombs?"

"Just wondered if, during your exploration of the neighborhood, you'd come across any and maybe taken a taste. The flavor from a honeycomb is—memorable."

Ayularc studied Mirah's face for a while. He let the sounds of the night occupy the awkward space between them. Then just as suddenly as the seagull took flight from its perch, he leaned back in the sofa and intently stared at her, eyebrows furrowing slightly.

"Listen, there is something you need to understand. Tonight's invitation had many reasons, but now after spending some time with you, I feel obligated to tell you of certain things that you undoubtedly have been made a part of. Granted, you personally may not have been directly responsible for your involvement; however, that does not negate the consequences stemming from your participation." He waited for a reaction from her, and just as fear started to caress Mirah like a warm embrace, he continued. "When you had those dreams and saw things from times you yourself had never witnessed in life, you were, well, your spirit was interacting with my world. For a human to reach our realm the way you did, it was something not done in a very long time. So you can imagine the warning alarm, so to speak, that was set off when you did."

Mirah heard his words but grappled to fully understand how she was able to do what was being described. She shuddered noticeably.

Ayularc reached her side in a heartbeat, stopping just short of offering a hug to stave off any of her fears. The memory of the pain experience when he touched her had him opt for a fur throw blanket, draping the back of the chair she sat on. Returning to the spot he was sitting, he continued.

"I believe somehow your body is—occupied with one like me. It is the only explanation for what is happening. The question is proving it and finding a way to remove the trespasser. But, the alarms are still going off as my kind are searching for the one among us whom you reached, as well as the human responsible."

"So you're telling me both of us are in deep, *deep* trouble? And that somehow, I'm possessed?" Mirah recoiled as coloring in her cheeks vanished, a look of fright now plastered on her face.

"Let's just say trouble is too light a word and possessed, ahh yes, you could use possessed. But the merging with you was not complete because you have remained in control for the most part. It is when you sleep; your spirit or subconscious is not strong enough to remain so." Waiting to see if she'd further react, Ayularc leaned forward again before speaking. "I need you to remember this conversation before you sleep tonight. I need your spirit to remember—me."

Mirah blinked hard, searching his face for an understanding of his request.

"When you go to sleep tonight, the other spirit will take control. Most likely, they will reach out to me in my realm and hopefully reveal what it is they want. But because you and I are running out of time, I will purposely locate you first and initiate the interrogation. If any of my kind finds you first, we can both say goodbye to the lives we know."

Mirah frantically unraveled her body out of the blanket. "I've got to go! She grabbed her handbag at the same time Ayularc stood; his frame seemed taller than she remembered. "This is madness, but I know enough to realize how real this *possession stuff* is," she finished.

"You don't fully understand the dangers after us. I think it would be better if you stayed here tonight. You will be safer here than anywhere else. Besides, you may have noticed that even for me, touching you is not pleasurable. I can only imagine what your focused energy would do to anyone else from my realm."

"Stay here? Are you serious?"

“Quite!” His tone had changed from that of kind and gentle to one which suited his statue and identity. The rush of his voice almost made her lose balance. Just as quickly, his expression changed back to the tender one from earlier. “You WILL be safer here. I have no reason to harm you, especially since you hold the answers to questions I’ll soon face. We need each other if we are to survive what’s coming. Now, I will show you to the room you will occupy.”

“I didn’t come prepared for a sleepover,” Mirah mumbled, following behind as instructed, knowing he was right. *At least he’ll protect me long enough to get whatever it is he feels I have locked away inside. God knows I don’t want to go back to my apartment tonight.*

“You will find clothes that fit in the closet and drawers. I’ve learned to keep a stocked house since living in this city; my business requires me always to be ready for anything. Feel free to utilize the adjoining bathroom. Don’t worry; I can assure you that you’ll have complete privacy. If you need anything, just call my name. I have extremely good hearing,” Ayularc turned slightly, opening the bedroom’s door while smiling at Mirah.

Mirah had followed the distance to the bedroom in silence, not wanting to know anything she’d probably not be able to deal with right then. She had enough to digest for one night.

Stepping into the room, Mirah's eyes focused on the bed's fluffy duvet. It looked like a large, inviting cloud. Ayularc remained in the doorway as she inspected the bathroom and looked about as if she thought someone might have been hiding, waiting for her to fall asleep. Satisfied with the accommodations, Mirah gave a thankful smile to him as he gently closed the door. Inside, the room became nearly silent. *He's most likely had the walls in this house heavily insulated. God only knows what goes on in here. Still, it is spotless, as if hardly anyone visits.*

Mirah opened the closet doors. Clothes of various sizes and designs hung neatly, spaced almost precisely apart. There were rows of shoes too along the floor. She opened some of the dresser drawers, not surprised by the packets of brand new underwear, sock, stockings. *He sure is serious about being prepared.*

Not long after, Mirah was chin deep in warm bubbly water. The huge soaker tub in the bathroom was hard to resist. Almost anything she could have needed was in the room. As she soaked, her mind replayed the conversations she'd had with Ayularc that evening. She questioned everything in prayer, but no answer came the way she'd hoped. All she could sense was a peace that was not her own. *And what's up with him not being able to touch me? Is it like some spiritual shield? If this is your doing Father, I am grateful. Knowing you are protecting me in some way is reassuring.* She stayed in the tub until she feared falling asleep and drowning.

Once out of the sudsy water, she welcomed the soft thick towel wrapped around her, retaining her body heat. She opted for a long pants pajama set, snuggling under the silk sheets and fluffy duvet before her feet got a chance to become colder.

The relaxing bath and welcoming bed made sleep not so hard to find for Mirah. The last thing she thought of before the blackness took over was how she would love a hot cup of chocolate, but the thought of moving from her warm spot coaxed her into remaining still. Soon her ears had only the rhythmic beating of her heart to break through the stillness of the room. Ayularc's face flashed in her mind before sleep carted her away.

CHAPTER 10

The heartbeat reverberated off of Ayularcs chest. Though Mirah was several rooms away, the insulated walls did little to muffle the sounds she made. He noted she'd been in the soaker tub for some time, though making a point not to listen to whatever she was saying. He knew she'd find bath irresistible; everyone did. Now that she was asleep, Ayularc became still in his own oversized bed. He was shirtless, wanting to expose as much of himself as possible to the air in order to sense, even with his flesh suit, any changes in the energy that whirled around Mirah. Within moments, his spirit was fully aware, walking in the realm of his kind.

He stood now in a memory of a time when his life was predictable. The view from the balcony of his home allowed his eyes to take in all the beauty of his land. His muscles tightened only to relax as familiar fingers walked up his back. The hands began to knead out knots in his neck as they massaged away his cares. *Don't get lost in the memory! This is not a pleasure trip. Get ready to extract whatever clues you can.*

"This view never gets old, does it?" Ayularc questioned the person whose hands continued to work his neck muscles. He did his best to act unaware of what was going on. *They can not know I'm on to them, not now. Not while I still have so many unanswered questions.*

"Ummm, yes it is, my love. Did you miss me?"

That voice. No denying it, not even after thousands of years. Trying to remain relaxed, Ayularc let his mind focus on happier days. Ones that were similar to this one. With all of his self-control, he stopped the hands from moving now onto his shoulders and slowly spun around. His breath caught at her beauty. She was radiant in the morning light. Hair black and shining like the oil from beneath the earth, framed a face, her eyes as blue as the skies. Blood red lips smiled at him. The smell of lavender undeniable, but worming through was the scent of sugared berries and warmed vanilla—Mirah.

Flashes of Mirah's face morphed over the beauty staring back at him. Mirah's spirit was fighting to remain in control, but Ayularc needed more time. He needed more time with Basielle—his wife long lost after The Flood.

"Basielle, my love! You look ageless." Ayularc cooed as he reached for a lock of her black tresses. He did this, knowing how she melted in his hands from such adoration. “This memory, it seems different,” he finished, hoping she’d take his baiting.

“My love, Yu Elle. Ahh, this memory, yes it was one of my favorites, don’t you remember? It was the day we were officially given rulership over this area. The day I become the queen of this land.”

“Hmmm, I remember my love. And the land as well as the fact that I loved you for the wise queen you were. Still, something seems different from what I recall of the day. Your touch feels so real, and the scent of lavender is strong, even for our realm.”

“Shhhh, my love. We don’t want to cause a scene. It would be unwise for anyone to discover what is happening between us.”

“What is this, Basielle? Our memories can not be manipulated to this extent, and if you were given a new flesh suit, I would have been informed. How is your spirit here? How were you called back from The Void?”

“Ayularc, always the strategist. You never could tolerate anyone outwitting you. Ahh, relax, my dear. All those years by your side served me well as I wondered formless in The Void. With no trace of my DNA to be connected to, there was little hope I’d ever be corporeal again. But man is weak, greedy, and selfish. These three traits were all that was required for me to gain access.”

"Gain access?"

"Yes, my love. I was able to gain access through the greed of a family's bloodline. All the person wanted was wealth and riches, of which I showed them where and how to get some."

"I don't understand, Basielle. Just what is it you've done because everything, my wife, that you do, the debt of which falls at my feet!"

"You concern yourself with debt?" Basielle shrieked. "I, my dear husband, was more concerned about living again. To return to a form of the life I once knew; the status, the power. I was trapped, tormented to what I felt was beyond the limits of my being. To make the unbearable even more so, we understood of the flesh suits being created for us. Some were able to be bound with them, while others became mad with the prospect of never having one. But to have that meant some remnants of our former self remained. All that I physically was and that of countless others have never been unearthed. I learned you were the first. A fact that had me believe my rescue from the endless suffering for sure was certain. Yet, time advanced for you while it remained looped for me." Mirah's eyes suddenly became a blazing red. Ayularc knew it was Basielle's doing.

Deciding to take a different approach, he pulled her closer. "This body, it doesn't do you justice, my love. Tell me how you were able to bind with it so we can figure out a way to have your spirit occupy a flesh suit customized, worthy of you." He paused long enough to see if there would be the slightest slip in her determination. Then, as she inhaled deeply, relaxing her shoulders, he pounced, "With you again by my side, we can continue to rule this place. There is much harvesting to be done, and when our kind reclaims all they've lost, my love you, my Basielle, will be the glorious queen of old!" Basielle fell limp in his embrace from the resounding confirmation she hoped for; to rule again. *Got you,* Ayularc thought as he squeezed her lovingly.

"Do you think it could be similar to what I looked like before?" Basielle asked softly, snuggling against Ayularc's neck, becoming lost in his touch.

"Certain features, yes. However, you may have noticed that we've refrained, at least for now, from creating our forms to be the height they once were. For the ease of moving about and carrying out our plans, we require the need to blend in as much as possible."

"Hmmm, I understand. I see you've chosen a shell that is similar yet different. It seems to suit this new persona you've adapted."

"Yes, I chose it for several reasons. It gains me the attention needed to be, ah, memorable. The humans I have regular dealings with respect a certain presence.

So tell me, how exactly did you bind with this body? Don't leave anything out; otherwise, I won't be able to help you." Ayularc's eyes poured on the charm.

Pulling away from him, Basielle took a few steps to enjoy the view. She dragged out the moments with her silence. Just before Ayularc was about to coax her more, she spoke.

"I had a lot of time to think of ways to break free from The Void. I methodically went through every memory about spiritual laws and those that govern our kind—nothing. Then I remembered hearing it said in The Void that there had been others who attempted to bind with humans. Many had no success, but there were a few who managed to complete the process. I bided my time, observing the interactions of man and the spirits trapped with me in that place which attempted the merging."

"Fascinating," Ayularc broke in.

"Yes, fascinating indeed. Still, the process required one to be worshiped. The human had to request our help, had to be willing to shed and pledge their bloodline to us. The pledge was mostly often done in exchange for wealth, long life, fame, some trivial thing that we knew would not be eternal. They were willing to trade eternal life for a flicker of the one they experience on Earth. A sweet trade if you ask me—for us I mean."

"So I assume you found a human desiring a trade?"

"I did! It was an ancestor of the woman whose skin I now ride. She was full of vanity, hahaha, she reminded me so much of myself. It was a perfect match. She asked for a long life and wealth. Based on the rules of merging, a human could only have one request. This is because the trade could only last up to four generations. Oh, hahahaha, she was a self-centered one. So," Basiell sang, spinning around to gaze again upon Ayularc, "I made the deal, stating that since she wanted so much, much more would be required in exchange."

"Just what was the *more* you required of her?"

"Ten generations. I calculated that it would be enough time for me to perfect the merging and find you, my beloved." Basielle's eyes dripped with desire for him.

"And did you? Perfect the merging, I mean?"

"Obviously not. Something blocks me from fully merging with this one. No matter how I try to force myself to complete the process, the pain of merging further drains me. It takes at least a year to regain my strength after each attempt."

"I see. And tell me, how many of the ten generations you required have you used up?"

"This is the ninth." Basielle sighed. "If I'm unable to figure out how to complete the merging, I'll have to wait for Mirah to have offspring and try the process all over again," Basielle continued, her voice laced with despair.

"So this bloodline must perpetuate in order for you to have a chance at merging?"

"Yes. Otherwise, I'll be forced to seek another willing to strike a bargain."

"Tell me, were merely words spoken to create the bloodline oath?"

"No, not words alone. The human must come into the agreement willingly, providing a sample of their blood or that of a living relative. An altar is made where the blood's poured out, and a piece of the altar is broken off, kept by the human making the deal, and passed on to relatives. This piece of the altar is the point of contact, my mark to claim them so that other spirits can't. Often it is kept and passed on as an heirloom through the ages. Some are fashioned into jewelry, artwork, sculpture, almost anything."

"My Basielle! If anyone could make this work, I know you'll find a way. Tell me, what does the piece of altar look like for this bloodline? And what happens if you are unable to complete the binding and this female has no children?"

Basielle's, face dropped slightly. She'd tried hard not to think of those "what ifs" of which Ayularc now reminds her.

"Unsuccessful merging and no children born of this female would mean returning to The Void. The altar piece was fashioned into a gold ring. The ring was passed on down the bloodline." Basielle indicated to the ring in Mirah's possession.

"But couldn't you bind with, say, one of her blood relatives?"

"No, my love. The agreement made was for more than one thing. Therefore, it is bound solely to direct descendants of the human that made the agreement with me from the start." Basielle sighed. "I knew the risks but was, I mean, I'm certain I can make it work. I just need to figure out a few more things. I'm almost there!" Fire returned to Basielle's eyes; her jawline became taught as she started to pace in front of Ayularc.

A tourmaline stone set in a gold band ring is exactly what Mirah was wearing! I have to convince Basielle to let me help her. The old Basielle would not fit well into the plan, my plan. The love I knew has no place in this new world, nor the one we are trying to create. She would demand being ruler over more than what has been allotted to me already. The counsel, Lu, for that matter, would hold me responsible for her bloodlust and uncontrollable rage. Such qualities had its place long ago, but the world has changed. Mankind has changed, and such recklessness could topple all that we've built, that I've built! No, she must not succeed—at any cost.

"You mentioned something; a force is blocking you from merging with this human. I've been toying with a theory for some time now. Many in The Void don't have any remains that can be located; no DNA trace to allow them to be bond a newly created flesh suit. But what you've done with the use of human blood sounds promising. I wonder if we took a sample of Mirah's blood and injected it into the created body if that would be enough for your spirit to bind with?" Ayularc thumb and index finger rested on his chin as he stared at nothing in particular.

"Hmmm interesting theory. I suppose it could work since blood is the lifeforce of humans. Not having her spirit in the way could make my merging easier." Basielle's small smile slowly morphed into a wide grin. "Genius! Just genius, my love. I had no doubt the two of us would figure this out. It's why I took the risk of reaching out to you like this previously."

"Yes, about that. We don't have much time. I'm not sure how much longer it will be before I'm discovered as the weak link. Mirah must be protected at all costs. Without her blood, we don't have a shot at making this work."

“And just how do you plan to get me a customized flesh suit without raising any suspicions?” Basielle questioned, now becoming more invested in the plan Ayularc had presented.

“Not a problem. I run this city and have my own loyalists within the group of those who create them. Over the years, I’ve established my own lab nearby. Only a select few will know what’s happening, and soon, my love, we will be together again.”

Basielle rushed Ayularc, arms wrapping around his neck, then feverishly kissing him. Expecting the agonizing shock of pain from touching Mirah’s body in such a way, he flinched only to feel nothing. *Of course, this is not the physical realm, so not all physical sensations are experienced here.* With that understanding, Ayularc kissed Basielle back. He was overcome by the mixture of scents, both Basielle’s and Mirah’s. His slender hands moved over her frame, but it was not that of the Basielle. The curves were of the woman, only a few doors down the hall from his bedroom. The human woman who had challenged him with just a gaze. The human woman he wished he could possess. Pushing away from the noise of his thoughts, Ayularc took advantage of the opportunity the embrace afforded, burning it to memory. Before her name could slip from his lips, Mirah woke up, leaving Ayularc painfully alone in his distant memory.

CHAPTER 11

Master.

Yes, Flyenz.

I've come to learn that there is still nothing to indicate The Fathers know how the connection was established. Nor do they know who the weak link is.

Good. Keep monitoring and report to me the moment something changes. I also need you to see about gathering fresh materials for a flesh suit to be made at my private lab. You know which technicians to contact. Tell them to be on standby, and oh, do remind them this is need to know—so no one else needs to know.

Of course, Master. How soon would you like the materials and everyone in place?

Preferably, within the week. I need that flesh suit grown and ready as soon as possible. How is Lu?

The Humtrack production has been his focus of late. Word in the ranks is that Lu expects to have several hundred each, under the command of the thousands being bound from The Void. New DNA samples have been coming in from across the earth, and he may be moving the time-table up a few months.

And my father?

He has his legion focusing everywhere but here, Master.

Good. At least he is doing his best to give me the precious time I need to fix this—wrinkle. Ayularc broke the connection between him and Flyenz. His flesh was focused on more nearby matters. He could sense she was awake but did as he promised and gave her privacy from his ears.

⌘⌘⌘⌘⌘⌘

Mirah's skin felt unusually hot, as if she was being pricked by countless needles. Heart pounding, she made quick of the distance from the bed to the shower. No time to fill the soaker tub; she needed to cool down.

With the flicking on of the bathroom light, her eyes slammed shut against the glare. Touch, smell, hearing, her senses were more heightened than she'd ever known them to be. The cool water from the showerhead stung as it sprayed her flesh, but soon it did as hoped. While her skin continued to cool under the downpour, she slowly opened her eyes again, allowing them to adjust to the lighting. She heard a gentle knock on the bedroom door. *How do I hear that with the sound of this shower filling my ears? There it is again!*

"Just a minute, please," she called out. She wasn't sure if it was Ayularc or maybe a butler or maid. No one else was seen last night while they talked, and the chef left them soon after they began eating.

Quickly she dried herself and grabbed the fluffy bathrobe. Satisfied with her reflection in the bathroom mirror, Mirah made her way to the bedroom door. She opened it just enough for her face to be seen poking out at the side.

Ayularc's eyes held hers. A warm smile on his lips and something uttered pertaining to sleep. Mirah was too lost in the vision of him, along with flashes of her dream.

Seeing she was not altogether paying attention, Ayularc loudly cleared his throat. "I was asking if you slept well and if you'd like something to eat?"

Blushing from embarrassment, Mirah clutched the neckline of the bathrobe, hidden behind the door.

"Sorry, umm, yes I slept well, I guess. Don't remember when I dozed off, to be honest. Hmmm, food sounds like a plan, hot coffee too?"

"Whatever you wish. I will have it prepared; you can join me on the upper level in say fifteen minutes?"

"Great, I'll be right there."

In a hurry to get dressed, Mirah had forgotten to ask what was on the menu. Well, it really didn't matter since she felt she could devour a house this morning. *No matter, I'll make do with whatever is prepared. Nothing so far in this place has been a disappointment.*

Ayularc smiled as he caught the last of her thoughts. Flyenz was very thorough in his reconnaissance. He'd provided many details about Mirah, including what she most frequently ate. Seeing her just then made him feel unsettled a little. He wondered just how much of her dream she remembered. Did she have any idea of what he was thinking? *We'll soon find out then, won't we?* Her scent tickled his nose, forcing him to think of his working plan to separate Basielle from her body instead of wanting to listen to her move about behind the closed room door.

He was standing before the large glass wall overlooking the bay in his living room when his gazing was interrupted.

Master, something has come up.

What is it, Flyenz?

The blog Mirah manages online got flagged, and one of Lu's sniffers has a team headed for her apartment. She's been making quite the disturbance in certain protected circles within the area. She is by no means the helpless one she can appear to be.

What else have you found out?

Nothing else, yet.

I want you to wait for them at Mirah's place. Be sure to note all of their actions and if anything is left behind in her apartment. Follow them once they leave, and the instant you know who their handler is, find out just how invested he is in his pursuit. If he can't be bought, slow his investigation down. I need more time.

Yes, Master.

The sound of Mirah's footsteps caused Ayularc to stiffen. *Moment of truth.*

"Umm, something smells good!"

"I took the liberty of having some of your favorites prepared."

"How did you...you know what, nevermind. I just appreciate the effort, and thank you." Mirah nodded, her empty stomach reminding her to be more gracious.

"You're most welcome. Thank me for what?"

"For allowing me a place to sleep while I continue to process all you represent. For all the questions I ever had about Biblical things, you are undeniable evidence. I am so happy I have my faith because, without it, I'd be a mental case right now."

Before he lost himself any further in the moment, Ayularc motioned for Mirah to ascend the staircase leading to the upper level. The dining table was beautifully set with several covered trays. A pitcher of fresh orange juice brightened the setting, but it was the hot pot of freshly brewed coffee that pulled her by the nose. This time they were alone, no server insight.

Seeing her realization, Ayularc interjected, "I thought you were more comfortable being alone with me, so I left instructions that we would serve ourselves unless, of course, you'd rather be served?"

"No, no, that's fine. I'm not used to being waited on, and yes, I'm not so afraid of you as I probably should be," Mirah replied with a raised eyebrow.

"Rightly you should–not, be so afraid of me," Ayularc said, trying to reassure her she was in good hands, a playful smile lightening his face. “Come on, let’s eat; I think between the two of us, there won’t be anything left of this delicious spread. The coffee, by the way, is all yours,” he winked while arranging his table napkin across his lap.

For a moment, Mirah saw him as just a man sitting down to have a wonderful breakfast with a friend. But he was not *just* a man. And what was their relationship, exactly? Everything she knew about his kind in Scripture and the many writings by those not canonized told her that whatever *this* was would not end well. Her grumbling stomach made her push down the rising anxiety as she filled her cup with the fragrant black brew.

⌘⌘⌘⌘⌘⌘

“Lu, we’ve found something!”

“What is it?”

“A blog by a human female who has garnered a fairly large following of people, all who are seeking the whereabouts of lost relatives.”

“And how does this fit into our current problem?” Lu questioned, shooting an annoyed glance at the figure before him.

"She mentioned in several communications with her followers about things she's seen in dreams. Things no human alive today should know about."

"And you think that she might be the one who reached our realm?"

"She certainly is a person of interest. We've also been able to put a timeline together based on physical and electronic trails that she has been investigating certain officials in her city who have *connections* with our underground network of Branded."

"Really?! Keep at it and get me more evidence. If she is indeed the one, I want to know who else knows and how this became possible. GOT IT!" Lu roared as he hit his thigh with a clenched fist. "You get a team working day and night on this. No one sleeps until I uncover the ones responsible for a possible breach of our realm and leaking of tactical information regarding our plans. We've waited too long to let anything stand in our way."

"Understood!"

"And should she prove to be the one we're looking for, I shall be the one to interrogate her. See that order is relayed to everyone."

"Right away, Lu."

Off in the distance, the birth sounds of another litter of Humtracks pleased Lu as he refocused his thoughts on the plans now in motion. Still, one trail of thought refused to fall in line with the others—who among them was the weak link. To betray them was suicidal. None would purposely allow themselves to be used in such a manner. Another thought branched off with an even more disturbing question. How then, could any of them become compromised, by a human at that? *It can not be one of my brothers; no, we were made higher than humans—but our offspring, only part of them have our imprint, the rest is HUMAN! So Brothers, which among you hides the identity of our betrayer?* Lu questioned in silence as he scanned the area. *The one who knows is here! Doesn't matter, all will be revealed, and this human's blood can be a useful ingredient in our plans. The creation of a new hybrid maybe? Hmmm, killing her may not be the most prudent choice. We'll have to find a way to keep her alive. Maintaining some form of control will be essential to the continuous provision of her blood.* Lu's eyes sparkled as a strategy budded.

A set of eyes watched him. Of late, they were always watching him, trying to discern what wicked scheme he was up to and if any of it involved his beloved son, Ayularc.

CHAPTER 12

Ancious eyes scanned the room. "Are you done with her laptop?" The man's voice was gruff and impatient.

"Yes, sir. The program's installed. We'll be able to see and record all of her online activity."

"Good. Okay, boys, make sure you leave everything the way you found it. We're out of here in three."

The short unsuspicious man walked to a nearby window. Glancing out, he noticed little movement in the street below. Stepping away, he dialed the contact on his phone, saved as Boss. An anxious voice answered, "Any updates?"

"We're about to leave the apartment now. All tracing software and devices have been installed."

"Alright, then. Report to me daily on your findings. I'll be periodically scanning the information dumped on the designated server."

"Yes, Boss!" The man replied as he signaled to the others in the apartment; it was time to get moving.

The group surveyed their areas, ensuring everything was as they found it before walking out of the apartment single filed, quiet. The hallway was deserted. Sounds of a stereo a few doors down helped to muffle their footsteps against the tiled floor. They'd picked the best time to get in and out based on scoping out the building, noting the daily routines of the tenants.

Once outside, without looking around, the group removed the orange safety cones from around their van parked right in front of the building's entrance. Each jumped in the open side door with toolboxes in hand. For the passerby, they just looked like a regular technician team from Big Boss Plumbing, as the words said, splashed across the backs of their uniform shirts and the sides of the dark blue van. Indeed the job was an easy one with no hitches and no witnesses. Well, none they could see.

Sitting in his car now just up the street from Mirah's apartment building in the same vehicle which had been following her weeks prior was a witness they would have wished wasn't there. Flyenz waited for the blue van to get almost past several more buildings before pulling out of his parking spot. He kept his distance and followed the them for about forty minutes until the van drove into a fenced yard. The sign on the building next to it read 'Big Boss Plumbing.' But it wasn't the sign's wording Flyenz noticed most; it was the image of a seal stamped in the lower right corner of the sign. The seal was one belonging to The Fathers. These were no doubt a group of Branded, or at least their leader was.

Master.

Go ahead.

Mirah's apartment was just visited by a group of Branded. The company cover used is called Big Boss Plumbing over on Roosevelt and 3rd. How would you like me to proceed?

Go back to the apartment and find out just what they planted. Most likely, there are cameras, so you'll have to just scan the rooms from outside the apartment itself. Check for a computer or laptop. I'm sure it's somewhere there and bugged. Do nothing else.

Yes, Master.

⌘⌘⌘⌘⌘⌘

The two of them eat their way through the delicious breakfast spread. Ayularc liked that Mirah had a good appetite and was not bashful about it. He had to all but secure a helping of the hashbrowns before Mirah spooned more onto her plate. She giggled at his facial expressions as she stacked an assortment of food in front of her.

"Don't judge. I use up a lot of calories for work." Ayularc shot her a questioning stare. "Listen, writing takes energy, okay?"

Ayularc held up his hands, indicating he surrendered, "I said nothing."

"Hmmm, but your eyes indicated you were thinking something about it, though."

"Guilty. BUT I was just admiring and pleased to see you have a healthy appetite. That's all," he chuckled. "Aren't you going to ask me?" Mouth still smiling, but eyes now serious.

Mirah's mood became less playful at the question. She'd hoped to drag out breakfast as long as possible, keeping things light and upbeat. But she knew there was going to come the time when the events which brought them together would have to be addressed. "Can't we enjoy this feast first? It would be a shame to lose our appetites prematurely."

"Of course we can. Think nothing more of it. Here, try some of this preserve. I make it myself from fresh berries."

"You cook?" Mirah couldn't hide her shock fast enough for Ayularc not to notice.

"I can, yes. Why does that surprise you?" Ayularc laughed, throwing his head back a little as Mirah's shocked face still stared at him.

"I mean, I guess it shouldn't. I'm sure you can do many things."

"Well, we are a hungry set, and I decided if I had to eat, I'd dine on more tasty things. Our metabolism was one that worked pretty quickly compared to yours. I'm not as hungry as I used to be, though. The flesh—bodies we now have, don't require that much food. Besides, I'm much shorter than I once was."

"Do you miss it? Your previous life, I mean?"

"Some of it. We certainly had more freedom, no need for hiding. But, I've come to enjoy the refinements of this age and the people," his words cut through her. The sharp breath she inhaled told him so.

"Don't you miss people from then? Your family, friends?"

“I have long gotten accustomed to the thought of never seeing some of them again. Yes, there are those I miss and others I’ve mourned. But many of them would not fit well into this age. They were not, let’s say, good at playing well with others. To walk among man now requires a lot of mental adjustments, composure, tact. Things that can not be taught but which require attaining from experience.”

“Do you feel? I mean, as humans do?”

“Oh, yes, we feel. Hmmm, imagine your emotions when they are at their most intense. That is how we feel emotions all the time. Well, whenever we allow ourselves to let emotions overcome us.”

“Let emotions overcome you? Do you mean you can stop them?”

“No, not stop them. We have, however, learned to control them, almost master them if you will. We call emotions humanity because they are uniquely human.” Ayularc noticed the slight confusion on Mirah’s face. “Ahh, okay, that may not be the best explanation. So, we call emotions humanity because The Creator also allowed man to be expressive with emotions, to give them and receive freely. Man has what my kind doesn’t, free will. If our humanity or emotions threaten to rise to the surface, if we have not all but mastered the ability to suppress them or allow them to increase while remaining in control, the results can be destructive.

Still, there are times when even the most skilled of us can lose control."

"So your anger unleashed is..."

"Frightening by human standards."

"And love, do you feel that too?"

Ayularc didn't respond for a moment. Instead, he pushed down on the memories threatening to make him come undone. Finding his voice again, he said, "love, yes, we feel love. We can love with a fierceness to match that of any human. Why do you ask?"

"To better understand to what lengths you'd go to accomplish something. I may not have said much, but I understand that there is an end game for your kind and mine. Since you have intense levels of emotions, it tells me that you can also be ruthless in your pursuits, which backs up the things I've learned through my faith." Mirah tried to lighten the mood, "and I'm grateful that you've offered to help me with whatever this is that's happening to me. I'd rather your *humanity* be used to help rather than come against me."

Slowly slender fingers retrieved the napkin from Ayularc's lap. He dabbed the corners of his mouth with the firm fabric, and while setting it on the table, he softly said, "for whatever reason, you and I have been forced together, know that I will do all in my power to keep you from harm's way. It's safe to say that not many of my kind would be so accommodating; they'd simply extract what they need from your mind and spirit, then be done with you. But for me, you are a mystery that I must solve. A ripple The Creator has placed in my waters. You, Mirah Drysen, have provided something I didn't realize was missing—purpose."

"Purpose? I don't understand?"

"My kind has a plan, a single purpose. I, like many others, have a role to play in the fulfillment of that plan. We have become only a portion of what and who we used to be. When I said I missed freedom, what I meant was the freedom to be—me. I want to rule this area that was given to me from the day of my adulthood, which *I am* doing now, but not freely. I need the advantage to raise even higher in the ranks. To be able to live without question. You, Mirah, somehow you will give me the edge I need to present, showing I am a necessary piece of the plan. More so than just for my scientific breakthroughs. It will solidify me as an indispensable one."

Mirah tried to take in all the information. Her mind sifted through Ayularc's words for key points. Then she found them, she understood.

"So, you need an advantage over other Nephilim rulers, something that will guarantee you remain corporeal. Am I correct?"

“Yes. Unlike our fathers, we offspring require a body to live in, to walk among men. New bodies are not to be created without the approval of The Fathers, and for any of us to get a replacement, we must prove ourselves a necessity; otherwise, our bodies are recycled and our spirits cast back into The Void. There are still so many of us who have yet to wear a new body. The Fathers reward replacements only for exceptionalism.”

“I see. So you can experience fear because it is ultimately the fear of losing what you have that is making you take time to work with me.”

“No, not just the fear,” Ayularc said, just loud enough for Mirah to hear.

“Oh? Then what other reason do you have?”

Wanting to shift the direction of Mirah’s questioning, Ayularc decided to drop the ax. “Basielle. I must undo the binding she’s done with your body. If she ever gains full control, her actions will not only mean a heavy debt I must pay, but she will try to rule again the way she once did—ruthlessly. This world is not prepared for her. The Fathers would not want her recklessness to expose them and their plans prematurely.”

“So the dream from last night, it was her that moved through me?”

"Yes, and she must not know that you are aware of what is happening. At least not until my plan is in motion."

"Great, glad to know *you* have a plan. Were you going to share it with me?"

"Yes, right after breakfast, remember? You were the one who didn't want to spoil our appetites, so I obliged."

"Yeah, I did, didn't I? Okay, so breakfast is officially over, spill it!"

Ayularc smiled with a raised eyebrow at Mirah's authoritative tone. "Would you prefer to go downstairs to talk or..."

"Here is fine. No more stalling," Mirah cut him off. Her face was still plastered in seriousness as she crossed her arms over her chest.

"As you wish, but I need to stretch my legs for a bit." Ayularc stood and walked over to the open ledge. A gust of wind swept up from the bay below, tossing his light-colored hair haphazardly about his head. Taming it with his fingers, he turned to look squarely at Mirah. "What I'm about to tell you can not in no way be recorded or shared? Do you understand?"

Mirah simply nodded.

Not satisfied she understood the gravity of the question, Ayularc asked again, only this time his voice bellowed with focus and force that it shook Mirah in her seat, "do you understand?"

Visibly shaken, Mirah's hands grabbed onto the sides of the chair as she wide-eyed Ayularc, color vanishing from her cheeks. "I, I under...stand," she stammered, giving him her full attention.

"Good," he replied, voice changed back to the gentler tone he was using before. "I needed to be certain. Even this morning your, apartment had a visit from a team sent to surveil you. You see, Mirah, the awareness of your dreams has set off a chain reaction within my realm, and I have the experience to know that we don't have much time before all is discovered. Oh, don't worry," Ayularc tried to reassure Mirah when her eyes opened wider, "I have someone looking over your place to see just what was done. That being said, I think it's best that you stay here, for now, agreed?"

Mirah was actually lost for words. A memorable moment. She tried frantically to think of a reason to disagree, but given the circumstances, she couldn't come up with a better alternative. *It's not like I can go to a friend's house with this hanging over me. I couldn't handle putting anyone innocent in the middle of this mess. Oh, Father, please keep me from all harm and danger. I know you have a plan for all of this. Help my faith Father to do as you instruct.* "Agreed," was all she could finally think to say.

"Okay, with that settled, let me give you a little back story on how you, of all people, ended up—here. About ten generations ago, so that would be, give or take almost seven hundred years, a female ancestor of yours desired what was not meant for her to have. Since no human could grant her the desires of her heart, she turned to spiritual means. In doing so, she was required to provide a blood offering. This sacrifice tied her bloodline, *your* bloodline, to the spirit which gave her what she asked.

Throughout the years since the covenant or agreement was made at that altar, the spirit has been looking for a way to take hold of a body in the bloodline. A body it could live in, control, take complete ownership. It's failed so far, but with you, it has found a measure of success. The problem is that of your bloodline; you are the most sincere in your faith. It is your relationship with The Creator, which keeps you, umm—shielded." Ayularc paused, not wanting Mirah to get lost in the information.

"Shielded, as in you touching me brings pain, shielded?"

"Yes, well, that's just part of what it means. You are shielded based on your faith, and anything not sent on behalf of The Creator that tries to connect with your spirit or body, unwilling by you, will experience difficulty, which is what the spirit now faces. It is not able to complete the binding process with you, so it can only manifest when you're sleeping. This spirit will not give up easily. I know first hand their determination, stubbornness."

"How? Who is this spirit?"

"Basielle, my long dead and lost wife."

Mirah's body went limp in the chair. Everything seemed to shift as the room started to spin, digested breakfast threatening to make an entrance forcing her to reach for a glass of water.

"Mirah, are you all right?"

She waved her free hand for him to continue while taking a long drink of the now warm water. *May as well have the bandaid quickly yanked all the way off instead of a slow peel.*

"If Basielle gains control of your body, things can go downhill quickly. Not only is your body not able to sustain her for nearly the number of years she'll demand of it, but The Fathers will see to it Basielle returns to The Void for not coming through proper channels as it were. Either scenario means you'll live the rest of your days in misery and succumb to either a drawn-out death or a swift one at the hands of a Humtrack."

"Hum...what?"

"Humtrack. It's a dog-spider hybrid used for tracking things in this world. One of Lu's prized experiments."

"Lu? As in..?"

"Yes, Lu, as in Lucifer. He sort of runs things. All the other fathers follow his lead and do their best to remain off of his radar."

"Whoa, it's really REAL. The Fallen—you call them The Fathers. Of course, from their mating with human women came you, the Nephelim. It's finally sunk in."

"There's more. I have a plan that can maybe rescue us from Lu's wrath. What Basielle's done to this point puts a lot of beings in trouble. We've got one shot. Are you in?"

"Am I in? I barely know what *being in* means? Okay, okay, just what, *exactly*, is your plan?"

"The details I dare not share with you. I'm not sure just how much of your memories are accessible by Basielle from your consciousness. I need you to trust me."

"Trust you!" Mirah said, more as a statement than a question. *Trust you,* she thought again to herself.

"Yes, trust me. Do you think He would have allowed you to spend so much time around me, if I were plotting something evil towards you?"

Mirah starred back hard into Ayularc's large pools. *He has a point. Up to this moment, I've not gotten any warnings in my spirit that he means me harm. But how could he not, when he's using humans for their blood and who knows what else. Father, what am I supposed to do here? I've got to get rid of this binding, and he's the only one who seems to have a clue as to how.* Mirah exhaled slowly and long. She waited a few more seconds before nodding her head in agreement.

"Wait, what about my job, and I still have stuff I need back at my apartment?"

"You can still go to work. Act as if nothing has changed. There will always be help nearby; you needn't worry. As for your apartment, I will have what you need to be brought here. Leave me a list."

"So, you're going to have me followed?"

"More like having you guarded, but you won't see them. They've been bred for such work."

"Are they...like you?"

"Like me? No, not exactly. Yes, they have bodies that look human, but their–abilities are tailor-made for surveillance and protection. Believe me; you won't even know they're around. No one and nothing will get close to you. The directive has been given," Ayularc flashed her a smile. One as sincere as he could make, holding it until he saw Mirah's body show the slightest sign of relaxing.

As tension slowly oozed out from a long exhale, Mirah gathered her bag and started for the door.

"The list?" Ayularc reminded her, all but shoving a small writing pad and pen in her path. His sudden movement caused Mirah to falter slightly from surprise. "I'm sorry, I must learn not to do that. I will move slower from now on."

A shaking hand took the items and began to scribble a short list. The most important thing was her laptop; all other things she would have written were creature comforts which she could do without listing since this house was stocked with them. She handed the pad and pen back to Ayularc, who'd stepped a few feet away so as not to crowd her.

"Right! See you around 6:30 PM?"

Mirah looked at him as if to say she didn't need a curfew.

"It's just best if you're indoors, here before dark. At night, they have the visual advantage over you, that's all,"

Ayularc assured her, "besides, by then, I should have more updates on how to fix this predicament we're in."

Realizing she had little choice, Mirah gave Ayularc a half-smile before leaving. The cool morning air pricked at her cheeks, and since she wasn't dressed as usual for office work, she opted to do some field investigation instead. There were some leads she wanted to check out that could relate to the recent rezoning efforts in the city.

CHAPTER 13

Scanning the notes of her Cloud saved document, Mirah began to make a diagram in the notebook kept in her car. She forced her mind to think of anything except for the last few days of her life. *No doubt, new money is behind the rezoning campaign for the Rizeen Towers building near the city's central park. If I can just make the connections, I may be...* The chilly temperature had warmed up a bit, but it was not the source of her increasing trembling. Her life had changed quickly, and though she knew there would be things discovered which would contribute more to that, she didn't, in any of her crazy-wild dreams, think she'd discover Ayularc and all that he represented.

Fear jolted her like unseen hands tightly gripping her shoulders, causing her heart's rhythm to lose a step. Clutching the fabric covering her chest, starting through her car's front windshield Mirah began to pray with fervor like that night she knew something was terribly wrong. That Tito would never have left and stayed gone, not without a message or phone call.

"Father, I trust you. I don't know how my research, marriage—Ayularc are all connected, but I know you have a purpose for my life. Help me to be bold in faith and walk this path. Help me not to let fear overshadow the peace and joy you bring. This binding thing, guide me through whatever comes next. Give me the strength to pass this test!" With a deep breath, Mirah closed her eyes for a few moments, then opened them once peace returned to her, focusing again on the notes her cell phone's screen displayed. She continued to scroll, stopping when her eyes came to a list of names who were noted as persons of interest.

A source who worked at City Hall passed on the list of names. They were of persons who may have the most to gain from the rezoning. The Rizeen Towers building was nearly built, but the project had shut down due to lack of funds needed to see it to completion. Many of the initial investors had all but gone bankrupt, getting the project to its current state. Word on the street was that the developer was open to *negotiating* with anyone who could help pay off the outstanding debts and get the building completed and sold for a minimal amount of profit.

"Abrams Court & Co., Manning & Sons, Alfred Daningshire, Bradock Limited, Spencer Hollings, A. Nephill, Byron Howa..., wait what? A. Nephill?" Mirah looked at the name on the list of investors; something about it wouldn't let her attention go. She rubbed her temple with a free hand, continuing to stare at the name.

Quickly she opened another browser window on her cell phone and did a property search with the name *Nephill;* three addresses appeared once the window refreshed. One she recognized immediately—her new home away from home! She entered the other two's addresses to get their directions. Taking note of them, Mirah decided to pay a visit to the one not far from the city line. The other was in a warehouse district, in a more secluded area, to which she was in no mood to venture to after knowing she was being observed, followed, *whatever*.

After responding to a few text messages from friends, Mirah started the drive following her phone's directions. The trip was a great distraction from the thoughts in her head. She turned on the stereo and chose the mini USB option, allowing the car to be engulfed with the praise and worship songs on her portable playlist. Soon she was feeling relaxed and excited about possibly getting some concrete proof of her suspicions. Someone, or something, was very active in moving influential people and things in the city like pieces on a board game.

Her mind focused on the melodies vibrating off of her body as the speakers pumped. The twenty-minute drive came to an end before her thoughts had time to drift out of line. The street was busy. She slowed, hoping to get a convenient parking spot. An old pickup truck started to reverse just then, and Mirah pulled up enough to allow it to leave before whipping her car into the space. Engine now off, she looked around and then in the direction of the building's large windows in front of her. She wasn't able to see much of what was going on inside since there was frosting on the windows blocking her view, reaching about three-quarters of the height of the window.

Deciding to get out and take a look around, Mirah grabbed her bag and notebook, then slowly paced a little ways from her car, taking in the area. The building was freestanding, and to its north side was an empty lot. Surrounding fencing and signs indicated it belonged to the city. As she turned toward the front tinted glass door, her stomach muscles tightened. There was something familiar about the place, but she couldn't quite figure out what.

A rush of cold air mixed with the scent of lingering cooking grease and cigarette smoke, along with the chime of a bell hanging dead center above the door, welcomed her upon pulling the handle outward. The ambiance was a mixture of arcade game sounds and patrons busy with their plates piled with items from the grill. Not a lot of people were inside, but that could be due to the fact it was still early. This place looked like it got the most action in the afternoon and evening. *These scents and sounds, I recognized them, but from where?*

Her eyes moved around the space; the few people nearby paid her no attention, of which she was thankful. Weaving her way through the arcade games, she pretended to be interested in one. Digging into her bag, she fished out a few quarters and tried her luck at the game. Fingers pounded buttons as she quickly racked up points, but her eyes made quick work surveilling the area near the rear. A set of double doors brought back the feeling of her nearly emptying her stomach's contents. *It was from that dream! And if my dream was based on reality, behind those doors would be...* Just thinking about what she'd smelt and seen in the dream made Mirah's stomach feel queasy.

She played another game, this time doing her best to drag out the clock. Using the time, Mirah continued to survey the place using reflective surfaces to see as many angles as possible. She hesitated to move from the game, biding her time to slip through the beckoning double doors. Spotting arrows indicating restrooms near her intended target, Mirah casually finished the game, grabbed her stuff, and walked in the direction of the sign pointing to the ladies' restroom.

She pulled her hair more toward the front of her face, hiding as best she could while taking slow-paced strides. A group of people entered just as she was a few feet away from the double doors. The commotion caused most heads to turn in the direction of the rowdy bunch. Seeing an opportunity to slip through the double doors, Mirah quickly pushed one forward, slipped through the small opening, and eased the door back to its original position, not wanting it to swing, showing movement.

A bright lit hallway caused Mirah's eyes to squeeze shut quickly. After slowly opening them to adjust to the brightness, she saw metal shelving with racks of supplies lined on one side. Mirah walked past them to see what else there was. A halfway opened door just beyond the shelving revealed an office, barely furnished save a desk, chair, and two filing cabinets. *Hmmm, no scents like in my dream back here. No evidence of blood or tortured bodies. Okay, so this IS the place in my dream, but if there are no people being kept against their will, what am I missing? Think Mirah!* As she replayed the dream, Mirah snuck back through the double doors and decided to use the restroom as a place to plan her next move.

Secure in one of the stalls, she flipped through her phone and looked at the other address for the warehouse district. It was close enough to the city, yet far away from heavily populated areas, so no one would notice or *hear* what was going on. A search online revealed that the warehouse building she was focused on and the other warehouse buildings surrounding it had the same tenant. *That's a lot of storage space for one company! A transportation company, huh? Just what do you transport Blue Light Trucking, I wonder?* The restroom's main door opened, then the one for a nearby stall, causing Mirah to hurriedly put her phone in her bag and quickly leave the room. As fast as she could exit the building without bringing too much attention to herself, Mirah made a beeline for her car.

Looking at the time on her car's clock, she had more than enough to go and check out the trucking company's address before sunset. *If this trucking company pans out to be the place of the rooms I saw in my dreams, the last thing I need is to be spotted. Do I want to take the chance of whoever is tracking me to know all the aces I have up my sleeve? But I need evidence if I'm going to expose these—whoever they are!*

The ringing of her cell phone made her jump. Laughing at herself, she pulled it from her bag and stared at the number. The caller ID glared back, *Unknown.* Mirah was accustomed to receiving blocked number calls in her line of work, so without much thought, she answered.

"Hello?" Her voice questioned as she tried to listen for any background sound before whoever was calling spoke.

"Having a nice day, I hope?" Ayularc's voice was unmistakable.

"Ahh, it's you! Don't you think the Unknown Caller is a bit much cloak and dagger?" Mirah tried to sound light-hearted to cover her thoughts. *I wonder if he knows what I've been up to this morning? Probably—cheezzz.*

"Hmmm, it has its advantages. Besides, you picked up, so that tells me your curiosity overrules your better judgment. Well, I just wanted to see how you're doing and to remind you..."

"Yes, yes, I know. Be back before dark."

"Yes, and that is BEFORE dark and not when it becomes dark. Please."

Ayularc's changing tone made Mirah question for a moment why the over show of concern for her. Or maybe it wasn't *her* he was concerned about.

"Don't worry; I won't let anything happen to myself or *Basielle*."

"Hmmm, you speak as if you want to ask a question or that you're assuming something. I can assure you, Mirah, your well-being is of great concern to me, even if your assumptions are misplaced. Both you and Basielle have important parts in my—plan. That's the other reason I'm calling. Given the current circumstances, it would be best if you stopped by your apartment and retrieved the items from the list you left with me. Don't want things to look out of the ordinary."

"But you said the place was bugged and being watched?"

"Exactly, and I have trusted eyes watching over you and looking out for anything or one who may put you in harm's way. I will advise, though, that you get in and out within ten minutes. No need to tarry, and oh, yes, do not turn on your laptop until you return to my house, understand?"

Mirah exhaled, hoping it would calm her nerves, now raw from the sudden rush of adrenaline due to her change in plans. She didn't do well with such disruptions to her well mapped out schedule. "Well, how will I know *your protection* is there, protecting me?"

"You won't, but believe me, they'll be there."

"And now? Are they protecting me now?" Mirah turned around in her car seat, brushing a lock of hair from her face, trying to spot anyone who may look like her protection. Nothing.

"Someone is always watching over you, Mirah. You have no idea how protected you are, do you?"

"I, well, I mean I know The Father watches over me, but still..."

"My thoughts exactly. You have no idea," Ayularc said, half smiling and longing for such watchfulness. "Soon, Mirah, much will be revealed to you, and many of your questions, doubts, and fears will be answered. See you by 6:30 pm." Ayularc hung up before she could riddle off the stream of questions biting at her lips.

Mirah gasped when she realized Ayularc had abruptly ended the call. Staring at the black screen of her cell phone, she said, "Okay, fine. Hang up then, but know this conversation isn't over. I will have my answers and if your plans or that of The Fathers has anything to do with this city's wellbeing, believe me, I'm going to expose it all." Just as she spoke the last words, a rushing heat rose from within her. Then in her spirit, she heard a low voice say,

"You will only do as I direct you. Some events must unfold."

Shaking from the correction, Mirah gripped the car's steering wheel until the heat evaporated from her body. Tears wiggled on her bottom eyelids, ready to fall with the slightest push. Instead, she used the sleeves of her top to wipe them away. For her to have time with traffic to investigate Blue Light Trucking and pick up a few things from her apartment, Mirah knew she'd never make it back to Ayularc's before sunset. *Fine, my apartment, it is. I'll just head out to Blue Light Trucking another day. Either way, I'm getting to the bottom of my dream!*

A sudden downpour caught her off guard. She didn't recall the news saying anything about rain, but the sizeable grey rain clouds in the sky said otherwise. When it rained in the city, everything seemed to move in slow motion. The narrow, congested streets became a chore to maneuver. *Good thing I'm not in too much of a rush.*

People were dashing into cars and doorways as the rain pounded mercilessly. At one point, it looked like sheets of light grey everywhere, forcing Mirah to drive the vehicle at a literal crawl pace. When she finally arrived at her apartment building, the rain had let up a bit. Dashing inside the lobby, she just missed knocking over one of her neighbors.

"Sorry, so sorry. Didn't see you there," Mirah gushed.

"It's okay, no harm done. This rain just came out of nowhere. Hey, haven't seen you online in a minute; everything okay?" Warren was one of Mirah's followers who also was suspicious of how events were happening in the city. He'd lost a few of his friends from his childhood neighborhood and noticed some of the panhandlers who frequently hung out on his mail delivery route had disappeared.

"Oh yeah, everything's good. I've just been busy, ahh, helping out a friend. Have you seen anything lately?" Mirah deflected.

"Nah, nothing lately but Mrs. Banner from 4A said some men in a van stopped by in the middle of the day yesterday. She wasn't sure what they were doing or which apartment they went to, but since they left here, TV and internet were giving her problems."

"Oh, really? Huh?" Mirah tried to look surprised by the news. Mrs. Banner's apartment was under hers; most likely, whatever was bugging her place was jamming Mrs. Banner's signal.

"Yeah, I told her I'd take a look later this evening to see if maybe she has a loose cable wire or something. I know that someone just rented vacant 7B last week, so maybe those guys went up to that apartment to do some work."

"Makes sense. Well, hey, you take care. I've got to run. We'll catch up, yes?"

"Yeah, sure thing. Just let me know when you're free."

Mirah smiled and waved as she rounded the corner heading for the stairs. She took them two at a time, wanting to avoid any more unnecessary questioning by her loving but nosey neighbors. Her hands trembled as she inserted her key in the lock of her apartment door. Slowly she began to open the door but decided against it. *You've got to act normal and not as if you know you're being watched.* With that thought, she pushed open the door, kicking it shut with her leg before plopping her bag down on the small dinette table.

Heading to the refrigerator, she tried to look for traces of intruders inconspicuously, but everything appeared to be in place, messy just as she'd left it. From the kitchen area, she downed a glass of orange juice while letting her eyes scan the apartment's open floor plan again. *You're wasting time! He said to only be in here for ten minutes. Grab your stuff and go!*

Heeding the reminder to herself, Mirah grabbed a few items and stuffed them in her backpack bag along with her laptop. She took her diary from the side table next to her bed and her favorite pair of sneakers from in front of her clothes closet. *One minute left, get a move on!* She laughed at herself this time because the voice in her head mimicked Ayularc. *Gosh, my thoughts are even sounding like him now, fussing at me. This whole situation just keeps getting better and better,* she thought sarcastically.

The moment she was heading down the hall to the stairs, her phone rang. Instinctively she answered, not bothering to see who was calling.

"You'd better be in your car!"

"I'm almost there. I had a run-in with a neighbor; well, I almost knocked them over, trying to avoid getting soaked by the rain."

“Yes, Warren Carter, 1A.”

“How did you—oh right, you have eyes on the building.”

“I make it a point to know all there is to know about anything that concerns me in this city. So you should be heading to my house then?”

“Yes. I had another stop in mind, but this rain put a damper on it. No pun intended.”

“Good, I’ll be there before you arrive. Do drive safely.”

“I will, thanks.” Mirah checked her phone’s screen. This time, Ayularc hadn’t abruptly hung up; instead, he waited for her to end the call. Smirking, she pressed the End Call button.

CHAPTER 14

Anything?

No, Master, Flyenz replied, *no one not belonging to the apartment building has been spotted.*

Did you place the scrambler in her car?

Yes, under the front passenger seat as you instructed.

Good. That should take care of any tracing while the laptop's in her car. The scrambler at the house will handle everything once the laptop is within its range. What about the other project?

The necessary personnel is on standby, and ingredients have already been assembled.

Alright then. Have the technicians begin the growth process. I will stop by tomorrow. Oh, and remind them to add accelerant. I need this body fully grown and ready before the next full moon.

As you wish, Master.

Ayularc continued to sit at the large table, none the wiser of his mental link conversation with Flyenz. He half-listened to the discussions now taking place around him again. The room of lobbyists, politicians, and investors reminded him so much of his former life when days were full of negotiating between clan leaders and territory overlords like himself. Nephilim overlords had trained their human subjects well in the art of negotiation. He smiled to see that the artform had successfully survived the ages. His standing ceased the heated dialogue that was starting to brew. All in favor of the takeover of Rizeen Towers had seen their future lineage through to great-grandchildren at least, be well taken care of from the deal. All Ayularc wanted to do now was be rid of them; his proposed buyout offer had them salivating. *Pity, none of them can be used for generating flesh suits.* He was sure their greed and lusts were imprinted in their DNA, an excellent complement to any of his kind who would wear their skins.

"Gentlemen, and ladies," Ayularc ceremoniously bowed, "I need to cut this meeting short. You all know what is expected of you in the coming weeks. The deadline has been set and failure, good people," he continued with a wicked grin, "is an unknown word in my vocabulary. Good day to you all." With that, he glided as if on air to the door of the private conference suite rented for their meeting. Once he was alone in the elevator heading to the lobby, his thoughts no longer became his own.

I understand they've possibly found the human.

Hello, Father. Yes, I'm aware and on top of the situation.

Well, I hope you know what you're doing. I suspect Lu is not far from discovering which of us is covering for his child in this mess. The tension here is more evident than usual. On another note, have you noticed the skies today?

I have. I take it the trial runs have been pushed up a bit?

Yes. Lu wanted to see how his new, improved litter of Humtracks compared to prior ones. He's enhanced their sense of smell for the Rh-negative blood. You wouldn't know by chance if the human has...

She does.

She? A female, hmmm. Don't let that become another issue for you Ayularc!

It won't. I have everything under control, Father.

Well, I'm sure you do, but....

Father, trust me. When I'm done with what I have to do, I will no doubt rise higher in the ranks. Believe me; I have no intentions of returning to The Void or losing all that I've reclaimed. This human holds the keys to more than I could have imagined and a solution for a past once lost.

What past? What are you talking about?

Relax, Father. Soon you will know and understand. The less I reveal to anyone else, the better chance of not being stopped. Go about your days as usual. I will let you know when I can share more details.

One thing, how do you plan to shield her from the Humtracks heightened sense of smell for her blood type?

By keeping her close to me.

WHAT?! Have you gone insane? Do you know there are eyes everywhere besides those of the Humtracks looking for her?

I do, and that's why she's safest with me.

Do you plan to torture me again in one of your many lifetimes? Arrrggg.

Relax, Father. If she is discovered with me, I will just say that I found her and was interrogating as to how the link became possible.

And have you found out how?

I will reveal all I know, Father when the time is right. Now, sorry but I really must go.

Ayularc. AYULARC! His father's voice bellowed in his head, but he ignored it. There was no way he was going to show his hand this soon. Not even to his father, who, after all, was not destined to roam The Void and could not imagine its horrors.

By the time he was pulling his car out of the building's covered parking garage, the skies had opened up again. Sheets of rain fell to the ground, filling potholes and making travel on foot treacherous. The streets were deserted of life, except for the metal kind like his car. Public transportation busses, ladened with passengers, pushed through the downpour. Red tail lights of vehicles ahead glared back like familiar red eyes. Ayularc decided to take a long way home, which would help him avoid the city streets' approaching congestion.

His mind skipped from thought to thought, decade to decade—all the things he'd done up to that moment. Yet, the past several days brought such an intense stirring in him; of all his experiences, he struggled to remember a time that could compare—then one came. It was his grip on the life he knew, which slipped away as the waters upon the earth continued to rise. His fingers now strained against the steering wheel of his car as they did to hold onto the protruding rocks in the cave that day. The sound of the rain and its life choking power made his face grimace. *I will not lose again as I did that day. My life will not be snatched from me! For whatever time my kind and Our Fathers have left on this Earth, I will live! And I will find again a resemblance of the pleasures and joy which have been so hard to keep buried inside.*

The familiar landscape told Ayularc he was almost home. The rain still poured but not as much as when he started the long drive. Several boats were making their way into the bay towards the docks just south of his property line. He loved the relative solitude this area gave him. A fluttering in his stomach took him off guard as he approached the last bend in the road to his home. A part of him hoped to see red metal parked in front, but it was just a fleeting notion. One quickly extinguished when rounded the bend, and his home came into full view.

After pulling into the garage, he waited for its door to close before stretching his long legs out of his car. He was in no particular rush and, for a moment, had no idea how he was going to entertain a human, Mirah, for however long she'd need to be under the protection of his roof. Humans served limited purposes for him, the women in particular. Yet, she was more than just another woman. She was an unknown, needed element to the masterpiece he was creating. She had somehow become the missing hue to the landscape he never knew he needed to surround himself with. Mirah. Unheard or thought of by him or anyone he knew until only a short time ago. Though much of life for his kind was predictable, it was the moments like these, those anomalies, that made living on the earth addictive.

Without paying much attention to anything, in particular, Ayularc motioned into the house, up to his bedroom, and into his shower on autopilot. The warm spray from his showerhead played a hypnotic beat against his skin. Thoughts of Basielle and all she meant to him filled his mind. He let his humanity drift on memories of her touch, her voice, her fire. If allowed to burn fully again, that same fire would turn his new world to ash.

The world is different now. What was required for their kind to move in and out of it today, Basielle would say, categorized them as the weaker ones and not the rulers they were born to be. No, as much as he desired to have her again, he cherished what he now had even more. Being stuck in The Void made one reevaluate importancies.

There are other pleasures to be had. You have the ability to make it possible to call any wandering spirit from The Void to be with you. Preferably one more malleable, his mind reminded him.

Ayularc's mind was still swimming in thoughts as he dressed. Memories of sunny days, unlike the wet and overcast skies, white-washing his current views. His sensitive ears picked up the sound of Mirah's car approaching. The hum of its tires riding on the private road to his home, the distinct purr of its engine. Quickly he fastened the buttons of his shirt. The shirt's fabric draped from his shoulders, tailored to accentuate his long lines and toned frame—the rich plum color contrasted against his flaxen hair and fair complexion. Pewter grey slacks completed his look, accessorized with a matching colored belt and loafers. The only scent he wore was that of a custom-blended shampoo, with notes of cedar's sweet citrus, rosemary's minty-pine, and the soft musk of vanilla clinging to his freshly washed hair. A few not completely dry tendrils made damp spots on his shirt.

Before she'd turned off the car's engine, Ayularc had opened the front door. He pointed to the rising electric garage door, indicating to Mirah that she was to park her car in the space next to his. The skies looked as if they had no intention of clearing, and it would be best if her car were seen as little as possible these days. Carefully, Mirah parked in the vacant space. The garage door closed just as she finished getting her belongings from her car.

"Need any help?" Ayularc asked, standing now in the doorway leading from the garage to the house.

"Ahh, no thanks. Not much to carry." Mirah glanced around the space as she stood up straight. Like everything else in the house, the garage was neat and tidy, everything in its place. Her eyes widened when they landed on Ayularc's car. The obsidian black sedan was shining under the overhead lighting. The car's sleek lines screamed to be touched. She tried not to gawk, but the love of anything automotive caused her to gaze longer than she'd planned.

"Sweet ride."

"It is. Maybe I can take you for a drive in it?"

"Maybe," Mirah's eyes still sparkled from looking at the treat when she finally looked at Ayularc.

"Hahaha," he laughed, seeing her facial expression, "oh, I think you'd rather *take me* for a drive than I drive you, am I correct?"

Mirah just gave him a confirming grin. She would most certainly love to take the fine specimen of machinery for a test drive. Feeling more assured of herself around him, she shoved her backpack into his arms as she neared where he stood, taking up his earlier offer to assist, brushing past him then to enter the house. The scent of his freshly washed hair arrested her.

Its fragrance, unique and mixed well with his scent, caused her to misstep. She regained her stride with a little effort, unsure which way to go, being on that side of the house.

"The second opening on the right leads to the foyer and stairs. I'm sure you can find your room from there," Ayularc offered playfully, not missing how his scent had stirred her.

Just outside the bedroom door, Mirah turned to wait for Ayularc so she could get her bag from him. On cue, he strolled toward her, arm extended.

"Is there anything, in particular, you'd like for dinner?" He asked, trying to surmise her mood, eyeing her intently.

"Ah, not really. I'm sure whatever is prepared will be delicious as always."

"Okay, then, that makes things easy," Ayularc flashed a mischievous grin, rubbing his hand together; licking his lips. "I've been in the mood for roasted chicken all day."

"Umm, that sounds lovely!"

"Good, because it should be ready in about two hours," Ayularc said with a slight smile. "I'll leave you to get settled. If you need me, just come downstairs to the living room." Without waiting for a response, he turned on his heels, walking towards the stairs.

Mirah wasn't sure just what he was up to, but Ayularc's body language was nothing but mixed signals. He seemed friendly and open at times, then, without warning, would become cold and distant. There was always an undercurrent of tension between them, even when she experienced moments of relaxation. *Whatever! I've got to figure out what's going on with me and the events that have hijacked my life. Ayularc and his agenda, I'm sure, will be exposed soon enough. A nice bubble bath is what I need right now.*

After filling the tub and adding contents from the first bath jar her hand touched, Mirah let her body soak in the fragrant water, suds tickling her shoulders as her mind tried to go blank. A melody skipped upward from her heart, and before long, she was humming the tune, riding the melodic waves. Visions of beautiful flowers in a field, the sound of voices and laughter nearby pulled Mirah deeper into a dream. The sun was warm against her cheeks as she spotted a bird floating on wind currents above. The ground began to vibrate under her feet where she stood. Faintly at first, slowly becoming stronger; rhythmic. The moment she felt she'd lose balance, it stopped. Her heart still pounded as she turned to see what was casting the massive shadow before her.

"Hello, little one." The voice bellowed, reverberating against her ears.

Mirah's eyes stretched wide as she took steps backward to take in all of the unbelievable sight. With neck tilted as far back as it could, she brought a hand up to shade her eyes from the brightness of the day. The face belonged to one she'd never seen before, but something about the smirk of the lips, the light-colored hair, and the eyes—those eyes whispered familiarity. Large orbs of dark brown, ringed in yellow gold, cut through her. Unable to speak now from her parched mouth, not attributed to the day's heat, Mirah starred back with a questioning look—*Ayularc?*

Her face spoke more loudly than he did. Knowing she must be in shock, unable to talk, he obliged with a head nod, slowly bending a knee until their faces were close. Close enough for her to feel him breathe her in with a long inhale. Unexpected rapping on the bathroom door stirred Mirah, causing her to splash some of the water over the tub's edge. She'd become so relaxed, falling asleep.

"Mirah, are you alright?" Ayularc stood extremely still, listening for any sound of movement. He'd given her privacy since leaving her outside the bedroom door, but when her heartbeat had become slower and faint, he took the stairs quickly, even for him. "Mirah, I'm coming in."

"Ahh, wait, no! I'm okay. Just dozed off for a minute in the tub, that's all."

Ayularc removed his hand from the door, continuing to listen for sounds of movement beyond it. Satisfied Mirah was not in danger; he let out a long sigh. "It was an area just beyond a place we called The Grove. I often went there to think."

Mirah held her chest; afraid her pounding heart would burst through on the next beat. *He knows? Was he experiencing the vision with me in real-time?*

"Get dressed. We have much to discuss," Ayularc stated before leaving the room, making sure to loudly close the bedroom door so Mirah would know she was once again alone.

CHAPTER 15

The rain still tapped against the walls of glass in the living room when Mirah descended the stairs. She was grateful for the warmth from the women's tracksuit's velour hanging in the bedroom closet. It fit just right and kept her comfortable against the chill in the air.

"Are you cold? I can adjust the temperature if you wish?" Ayularc questioned, noticing her outfit of choice and the fact the jacket was zipped all the way up.

"No, thanks. I actually like it. Much better than melting in the heat. Besides, this weather and the cool temperature is guaranteed to make me sleep quite sound tonight, despite the nap I pulled off in the tub." Mirah gave him a playful smile. "So, why exactly did you come knocking on the bathroom door? And what was that about The Grove?"

Ayularc looked at her for a moment; then, with the blink of his long eyelashes, he gestured for Mirah to take a seat. She opted for the chair again, this time tucking her feet under herself and grabbing a throw pillow. Once she appeared comfortable and settled, Ayularc walked to the glass wall of windows and stared up at the skies, darkened now by more rain clouds. With his back still to Mirah, he searched for words to paint what had become her new reality. From the corner of his eye, he could see her reflection in the window. *She looks so vulnerable—such easy prey.* Pushing the thoughts aside, he turned and took a seat on the rug at her feet.

Mirah was a little unnerved by his seating choice but swallowed hard to calm her emotions. It seemed like a long time before either of them moved, just sitting, staring at each other as their chests rose and fell with each breath. Ayularc broke the silence when he saw Mirah's mouth about to speak.

"I came to check on you because I could no longer hear movement in the rooms. I knew you were in the bathroom, and I was concerned something had happened to you."

"People go to the bathroom all the time and are quiet, so I don't follow your reasoning? Besides, I thought this would be one place I'd be safe?"

"Yes, but when someone's heart slows, and they aren't making any sounds, that would be cause for—concern, would it not?"

"Wait, my heartbeat slowed? How slow are you talking?"

"Very, *very* slow. Listen, you are safer here or in my company than anywhere else; yes, however, there are certain things that even I can not protect you from."

"Such as?"

"Such as your heart-stopping or you bleeding out from a slip and fall. I have abilities, but they are not for regenerating of your kind."

"Okay, but wait, I still don't understand why my heartbeat would get so low that it would freak even you out."

Ayularc decided to take a different approach. "You mentioned The Grove. Well, apparently, your heartbeat gets very low whenever you have connected with me or my past—umm, whenever you walk the plane of my kind."

"Hold on. You mean that *you were* in my dream just now?"

"Ahh, you can say my spirit was aware of you. Physically, I was here watching the rain, but not in so many words, yes, I was aware of what you were seeing, experiencing."

"So are you saying we are somehow linked? But we've made no covenant, and I would remember if we slept together, so that's out of the question."

"You're right. You and I haven't made a covenant, but the one with Basielle and I has managed to remain, even after all this time. Plus, the fact that your bloodline has made an agreement with her means you, in essence, are connected to her. Thus I believe, somehow also connected to me." Ayularc reached for Mirah's knees as he saw her face begin to lose color. "Breathe Mirah, breathe. That's it, deep breaths."

"I need a minute," she gasped, eyes noticing his hands on her knees. But this time, he hadn't flinched in pain, nor had he moved them away. "How is it you're able to touch me?"

"I'm not sure. Maybe because your defenses are down. Spiritually they were up when we first met, and since then, I noticed they fluctuate based on your current frame of mind. Don't worry, I can sense when it's best I keep my distance," Ayularc added with a sincere smile.

"Good to know," Mirah said, mind now sifting through information. "Okay, so I somehow see your past." Ayularc nodded in agreement. "And I'm also having dreams of the city, the world, but they take place in this time period," Mirah paused. "I wrote them down in my journal, things I've seen in my dreams," she continued, motioning that she wanted to retrieve it from the upstairs bedroom.

"You stay here and try to remain relaxed. I'll get it." Before Mirah could object, Ayularc was already nearing the stairs, and, after a few moments, he was sitting again on the rug before her, handing the journal to Mirah, whose face was trying to become accustomed to his inhumane speed.

Shaking her head to focus on the now, Mirah flipped the pages to look over the notes of dreams she'd been having for the past six months. As she read them off for Ayularc, he seemed surprised at times; then a bit saddened realizing she had been privy to so many things unintended for any human to know unless spoon-fed on purpose with the approval of Lu. Her knowledge of these things meant she was more of a risk to his kind than he'd previously realized.

"The dreams you've just read about have many key elements that pertain to future events. All I can say is that you should not know these things, and especially now, you shouldn't tell anyone else about them. Do you understand?"

"Well, no, I don't. I mean, The Father gives us, me, dreams and visions to let us know things that are important. Information we use to help prepare or prevent things from happening. Why wouldn't I share with others the events that are coming!" Mirah's voice began to rise in frustrated confusion.

"You shouldn't share this information because the ones who sent people to track and monitor you have the ability to do more than that."

"Oh, really? So what, they're going to make me disappear or something?"

"Or something!" Ayularc saw the flash of fear come over her. Quickly he tried to settle her mind because he started to feel pricking pains in his hands as her defenses began to rise. "However, I have a plan to make you appear to be less of a threat, but first, we eat!"

Food, yes, food! I'm going to need a full stomach to get through this night, I can already tell. Mirah thought as she followed Ayularc to the upper-level dining area.

⌘⌘⌘⌘⌘⌘

"Updates!"

"Nothing much, sir. She came home just before dusk and took a few things then left."

"Clothing? Anything to indicate she wasn't coming back for a while?"

"No, nothing like that. She just took her laptop, some books, and papers."

"Alright, then. If she's not home, at least we can track her laptop. I want to know the minute she powers that thing up, you hear me? The minute!"

"Yes, sir!"

I can't afford to mess this up! This seemed like a simple enough job, and my skin is riding on bringing back intel on this woman. Shhh, from the looks of her in photographs, she would have been an easy snatch and grab. But, who am I to argue with Boss. He said monitor and track and so help me; if these clowns botch this up, my skin will not be the only one hanging out to dry!

"Sir, we're ordering pizza; you want some?"

"Yeah, extra pepperoni and a diet cola."

Still staring at the photo of Mirah on his phone, the leader of this team wondered, *what is it she's got on these people? I haven't seen them so antsy before. Whatever it is, I, for one, am glad not to be her. I heard from others around the city that they don't give second chances, and what I've witnessed confirms it.*

The man shuddered as he recalled the last time he was at a meeting with Boss and a few of his associates.

The other attendees didn't like the terms of the agreement and wanted to prove a point. The last thing they remembered or felt was something black and sharp pointing at them before poking out the other side of their bodies. That thing still gives him nightmares. *Was that a dog or a spider? Blacker than black and mutated, ugly as all out! I know that Boss dabbled in genetics, but man, that thing doesn't need to be reproducing.*

He turned his attention to the small TV in the far corner of the room with a shiver. The weather was being discussed, and video footage of the skies across the city was being shown. "Crazy weather," he murmured, dialing his wife's number in his cell. He promised her he was only a gig or two away from getting out of this hustler life. But the truth is, he was in deep.

Separation from Boss meant *separation* from everything and everyone—permanently. He'd tried to explain that to her, but she refused to believe it. To compensate for her waiting and distract from reality, he showered her with gifts and vacations anywhere she desired. Yet, he knew soon, such would no longer keep her content. Boss demanded complete loyalty, even from the families attached to his workforce. No one was beyond his reach—no one.

CHAPTER 16

That dinner was the quietest meal Ayularc and Mirah had to that point. Each toyed with thoughts and questions while eating, picking at the wonderful spread before them. As usual, Ayularc's staff had made another mouth-watering meal. Though Mirah's stomach most certainly welcomed it, her heart and mind were far removed from the experience.

There's no easy way to explain what horrors are headed her way, so why be indirect about it? Because, if she's spooked, she may do something crazy like posting everything on her blog or, worse, somehow weaving it into a piece for her column at work. No, need to take cautious steps, control as much of the emotional flow she's bound to have as possible. She's more powerful than she realizes, and that strength can work to our advantage. Hmmm, yes, I need to teach her how to harness it. For her to not only use it for self-defense, but also for unbinding with Basielle. Just have to make sure she doesn't become uncontrollable for me. Got to move fast. Her little nap charged her so much she even connected with me after only a short period of time. Mirah's spiritual activity is increasing, and the more active she becomes, the easier a target we'll both be.

"If you're done eating, we can continue our discussion downstairs."

"Yes, I'm full, thanks. Would it be possible for me to have a cup of hot tea?"

"Not at all. A cup of tea sounds delightful. I have a tasty berry blend I'm sure you'll like."

"Ummm, sound perfect, thanks."

"Good. Why don't you go on down, and I'll bring the tea in a few?"

Mirah smiled and nodded as she rose from the table and stretched. She had to admit, it was great to be catered to, have meals prepared, and no dishes our house to clean. *Don't get too comfortable here. This is temporary, and besides, don't forget what he is. Keep your head on a swivel and your emotions in chains!* Heeding her own warning, Mirah straightened the tracksuit top and descended the stairs heading towards the living room.

The rain had stopped, but the skies were still overcast. No stars could be seen, and the moonlight was nearly hidden. It felt as if all of nature had stopped moving. Small hairs at the back of her neck raised as she looked outside the wall of glass windows. She felt as if something or someone was staring back at her from the other side. But all she could see nothing more than the water of the bay and the landmass far on the other side. She shook her head as if playing off the eerie feeling, and instead of plopping down in the big chair she'd fallen in love with, she opted for an end of the sofa near a tall vase, using it to help shield her from the sensation of an observer.

Ayularc appeared sometime later with a tray laden with a tea set. He noticed Mirah's seating selection and placed the tray on a folding table he'd had tucked under his arm. He could sense a change in her. Fear, no, she felt uneasy, exposed—her spiritual sensitivity was high, something external was the cause this time.

"What is it?"

Mirah looked up at him, not daring to turn her gaze anywhere near the windows. "I feel as if I'm being watched from out there," she said, tilting her head towards the vase, her shield from the wall of glass.

Ayularc motioned to a panel just below the sofa's back, and with the press of a button, white, almost iridescent blinds lowered from an opening in the ceiling. "I can assure you, no one is watching you." Seeing the unspoken question still in her eyes, he continued, "and nothing dare invade the privacy of my home."

"Something is out there!" Mirah said assuredly, "I can feel it," she finished in almost a whisper.

Ayularc knew she was right, but he wasn't ready yet to expose her to all that went on around her. He needed to know she could handle the reality of the world. That it didn't function the way, many humans believed. To lighten the mood, he offered her a cup of tea. He was sure the scent of the blend would lift her spirits in a more positive way. Besides, if she remained on guard, he'd be in for a painful night when trying to lay the foundation of all he needed her to know.

"So tell me, what do you make of the dream notes you read for me earlier?"

Taking a long sip of her tea, Mirah mentally went over the notes trying to put them in order based on what's happened in the city so far.

"Well, I know the dreams were not of the past."

"What makes you believe that?"

"For one, the chaos in the city I saw has not happened yet, neither anything like it from my research of the area's history. Then there is the dinner arcade, which I did, by the way, find and checked out. I was able to access the back area of the building but found nothing like the torture rooms in my dream. Still, in my dreams, you were there, so..."

"So, think. Could the dream have been showing you two different places that your mind assumed were one and the same? If you didn't see me there, then that could mean there is another location, right?"

"Yes, that would make sense. Also, there is another address I was going to check out before you let me know my place was bugged and insisted I get here before sunset."

"Oh, you have another lead?"

"Yes. At first, I thought it might not be much, but now that you've given me a different perspective on things, it would make sense to have such a location used for the torture I saw. But how do you tie into all of this?"

"That's a good question," Ayularc said with a raised eyebrow. "You didn't mention the other location's whereabouts. Is it another place in the city?"

"No. It's a warehouse district out by the edge of the city."

"Ah, I see. Hmmm, what made you connect it to the dinner. There must have been something that made you do it?"

"There is. They both have connections with some affluent people in the city. Plus, I came across a name on a shortlist which caused warning sirens to go off in my head."

"A name?"

"Since you're so *connected,* maybe you could help me find out more about them. All I have is an A. Nephill. Sound familiar?"

Ayularc rested the teacup in its saucer without so much as a hesitation upon hearing the initial and surname. He could feel Mirah's eyes on him, looking for the slightest change in his demeanor, similar to the way he looks at her for changes in hers. Once the teacup was properly balanced, he looked up at Mirah.

"I recognize the name, yes. It is the one I'm currently using. I can also tell you that the other names on your list are not one to be *investigated*. Take my advice and drop it."

"Is it because they are like you, a Nephilim?" Mirah pushed, determined to get some answers.

Ayularc flashed her a slight smile before becoming serious again. "No, they are not like *me*. They are merely a puppet. We call them Branded. It is the puppeteer who holds all the power. *They* are the one I'm trying to protect you from."

“That’s not good enough! I need to know what’s going on, and if you can, do shed any light on things. PLEASE, please, tell me.” Mirah’s eyes were now wide with desperation. Ayularc felt a pull on his humanity, cursing the way she was starting to unravel him, again.

“I will do what I can to ease the discomfort of your mind, BUT whatever I reveal, YOU MUST NOT share with anyone else. There is much more at stake than your blog or job.” Ayularc paused to let his warning take root. “Lives and souls are up for grabs, literally. Understand?”

Mirah shook her head rapidly, half in fear of what hornet's nest she just kicked and half in relief that she was not crazy or headed in that direction.

“Branded are humans who have, as humans put it, sold their souls to the devil for whatever desires they have. All of which are temporary since humans don’t live in their current form for eternity. These Branded, conduct business on behalf of the one they made a deal with. And no, it is not The Devil. They are actually making agreements with one of The Fathers.

Whenever our kind needs something done that requires a human touch, a Father is found that has a Branded under his control who can get the deed done. Make no mistake, these Branded are human, but also much more in a sense they have no consciousness remaining. To seal the agreement with a Father, a

Branded has to do unthinkable acts—regularly. Over time, the human consciousness becomes seared and callous, unable to distinguish right from wrong, only able to feed its unquenchable hunger for self-indulgence.

If a Branded is compromised and their allegiance discovered by another human, the Branded and all who may have knowledge of the agreement, the way The Fathers operate through humans are taken out, destroyed, and all traces of them gone forever.

Another thing, this fluke in weather is the signal that the next wave of our kind's plan is beginning. The dream of the father and son being taken, that has been happening for a very long time but not in the way you saw in your dream. Remember the weird clouds you saw them being pulled up into?" Mirah nodded, not taking her eyes off of Ayularc, not wanting to miss anything his body language would give away. "Those clouds are here, outside right now, producing this crazy amount of rain as a disguise. Soon people will be taken directly, during the day, at night, whenever they want. No longer as before in secret."

"Okay, got it. Stay away from any Branded. Wait, what do you mean by people have been taken for a long time now? And taken for what, exactly?"

"People have been taken off the streets, as favors to those in power, wanting someone to *disappear*.

Random ones who live alone or have no family to miss them. These were being literally snatched and held hostage."

"Held hostage for what? It's not like they have a lot of money to trade; nothing valuable."

"But they do—have something of value. Themselves."

Mirah jerked back at the statement. Her stomach flipped at the words as they repeated in her head. *Tito! Could this snatching have happened to him? Was he still alive somewhere, a hostage?*

Ayularc waited until he had her full attention again. He could see from the darting of her eyes, she was lost in thought. "The human body is precious and unique. Those humans in particular, with a rare blood type. It is a blood type that we are able to use to make our flesh suits and keep them functioning. But it is rare, and so those who possess it are handled with much care and discretely."

"Rh-negative," Mirah whispered. "The same as mine. Does this mean they'll come to make me a hostage too?"

Ayularc didn't respond at first. He wanted to be sure he used the best words in this situation. Still uncertain with just how much of his plan he could trust her with, he decided to provide only what was beneficial—to him. He needed to stretch his legs. Taking long strides to the windows, he pulled at one of the blinds to peer out into the night. To human eyes, the bay and surrounding landscape were soulless, but to his gold circled, dark irises, there was an abundance of activity happening all around them. Activity, for the most part, that wasn't paying him too much attention, and it was just how he wanted to keep things.

"No, they won't come for you, Mirah. Not in the sense of you being taken as a hostage. But hostage really isn't the correct term, don't you think," his breath fogged the glass as he spoke.

"What do you mean? You said people are taken as hostages."

"I used that word in hopes you'd correct me. Think, Mirah—hard. Remember your dream..."

She stared at the back of his head as if trying to pry from it the clues he was hiding from her. *My dream...yes, my dream. Ayularc was in one of the rooms with that man. He was drained of his blood, something about them needing it to power their machines....machines, oh, he meant their flesh suits.* "Sooooo, wait, the people being taken are not hostages but, they're a blood supply!"

"Blood AND flesh or DNA supply to be exact," Ayularc added to help fill in the missing pieces to her jigsaw puzzle. He turned in time to witness her gasp at the revelation. Her face was starting to glow now, from the clarity this information provided.

"So I was being shown what is happening and about to happen? If this is so, what role do you play in all of it?"

"My role, I will share with you soon, but what you need to understand now is that my kind is looking for you, not for your blood, but to learn how you're able to reach one of us spiritually. They will do more than use you for blood and flesh, far worse. I need to understand why and how you reached me, of all Nephilim." *Well, I do have a theory, but I will only share once I know it can be reversed.*

"But to give you some insight as to why you saw me in your dream, I do, as mentioned before, play a significant role in the binding of bodiless spirits from The Void. My DNA helped make the blueprint, if you will, of the process. In this city, I have a vested interest in the smooth in and outflow of not only information but also that of Rh-negative humans."

Mirah's face went ghostly white. She feared that being with Ayularc would mean, at any moment, she'd end up as source material for some wicked experiments. Her thoughts were evident with each passing moment. The bass drum sound of her heart rang loudly in Ayularc's ears.

“Relax. You are safe here. I said nothing would happen to you, and I intend to make sure of it. Besides, you are more valuable alive than anyone else. You are an enigma, something I never thought I’d find again.”

Seeing the moment as an opening to pry deeper into Ayularc, Mirah allowed the question to roll off her tongue. “And what happens if your plan to separate me from Basielle doesn't work or if somehow I’m found by The Fathers? The truth Ayularc. I have to know what I’m up against.”

Ayularc took the chance that touching her would be safe or at least bearable at that moment. Cautiously he reached for a free hand and upon contact was happy to feel nothing but a tingling sensation instead of a painful jolt.

“If, IF, you are found by The Fathers, then you will be subjected to countless attempts to connect with them. They will probe your memories and thoughts to discover all you know. The experience will not be as it is when you and I connect. Remember, I’m only half of what they are, and they are very good at what they do. They lack the level of humanity we Nephilim possess—they are ruthless.

So you see, separating you from Basielle has to be a success. I don’t know how much longer you will remain, *you* or when Basielle will realize that remaining with you keeps her limited in this current state. Either way, your body can not contain her spirit for too long. He saw no change in Mirah's expression as he spoke. Her ears were open, and heard all that was said, but a glaze had come over her eyes. She was reflecting, distancing herself from any emotional trigger his words may form. The tingling sensation was becoming stronger; pain started to increase. *She's praying!* Ayularc quickly withdrew his hand from Mirah's and stood, taking a few steps back to give her powerful essence space to expand.

Deep in Mirah's spirit, a fire started to burn. Its heat crawled like thousands of fire ants out toward her skin. A blaze ignited, and it felt as if flames licked at the space surrounding her body. She felt it as it pushed Ayularc away from her, expanding still. In her mind's eye, she could see herself sitting on the sofa surrounded by the glow of white, and golden-orange light. When the edges had expanded about three feet around her, it quickly contracted again, into the center of her chest. The room appeared as it was before, except she was able to glimpse for a brief moment, Ayularc's spirit recoiling from the display of her spiritual power. *He fears me, at least a little!*

Ayularc recoiled almost noticeably from the demonstration of Mirah's spiritual power. He needed space. Space away from her. This plan of his was risky, but he saw no alternative to having her nearby, and under his roof was the safest place he could think of for her to remain. He needed to up his schedule and somehow get to dislodging Basielle from Mirah. But how? A flesh suit was a long time away from being ready, and without one.....*wait a minute. Basielle doesn't know the process of creating one, and she has no other to communicate with to compare the difference between a custom flesh suit or an ordinary human. I just need a body to have on display. It must be beautiful too; otherwise, she will insist it be remade.* Ayularc's eyes twinkled with amusement, throwing the onlooking Mirah off.

"What's funny?" Mirah asked, now standing and stretching her legs, which had cramped from being sat on.

"Oh, not funny, but brilliant. Mirah, I believe I've found a way to accelerate your freedom from Basielle. Come, you need to sleep, and I have a call to make. With a little midnight oil burning over the next few days, we may be able to get things underway." Ayularc said, ushering Mirah toward the stairs. He followed, making sure to remain a few feet behind.

Once she was in her room, he went back down the stairs. His feet made little sound as he took the corridor toward the garage. He touched the wall on a spot just beyond his reach. It was intentional as even he, with his stature, had to get on tiptoe to reach it. An opening appeared in the wall next to him. Once he'd stepped through, the opening closed, and the wall appeared as before. Automatic lumination filled the space, which was the same size as his garage. The hidden room contained his private collection of experiment data, jars, and vials of samples he'd worked on through the decades. Standing near a desk off to the right side of the room, he swiped his finger over the touch screen of a laptop.

Fylenz!

Yes, Master?

New assignment. I need you to find me a female human to fill in for a newly created flesh suit. She'd need to be at least 5' 10", any shorter, and there could be complications. Her hair needs to be brunette, and facial features must be beautiful—breathtakingly beautiful. Understood?

Understood, Master. Is she to be delivered awake?

No. Drug her and be careful she won't be missed. I may need her for a few days. When you've found her, send me a photo for approval. And Flyenz, burn the midnight oil on this, okay?

Yes, Master, as you wish.

CHAPTER 17

Mirah's cell phone showed two missed calls from the same number and one voicemail. The caller ID showed it to belong to the local police department. With shaking hands, she played the voicemail.

"Good evening, Mrs. Maurez. My name is Detective Sykes, and I've been investigating an incident that involved your husband, Tito Maurez. Please give me a call at your earliest convenience to go over some important information. My number is..." Mirah's ears became deafened by the repeating statement of Detective Sykes *investigating an incident which involved your husband...*

She looked down at the phone, the black numbers going in and out of focus as tears blurred her vision. Part of her was relieved to know anything about Tito; the other was cemented in place, not daring to learn of anything unthinkable. Knowing she'd not sleep now with this new development, Mirah took a chance to call the Detective. The call was picked up after only two rings.

"Detective Sykes."

"Ahh, yes, hello, Detective Sykes. This is Mirah Maurez returning your call. Sorry for the late hour, but I wouldn't be able to sleep..."

"That's quite alright," the detective said, cutting off her apology. "I'm glad you called. I know it's late, but is it possible for you to come down to the station, if not tonight, early tomorrow morning? It shouldn't take long to go over a few things."

"Ahh, umm, yes, of course. I can be there in about forty minutes."

"Okay then, I'll let the desk sergeant know; just ask for me when you arrive. See you soon."

"Sure, yes, and thank you," Mirah said before ending the call. Arms dropping to her sides as she braced herself for whatever awaited her. *He didn't sound cheerful, as if he has good news for me. Oh, Tito, what did you do? Why did you just leave so hot-headed? We could have worked it out!*

She looked at her reflection in the bedroom mirror. Her outfit would do; she just needed an outer jacket or coat and a change of footwear. By the time she made it downstairs, Ayularc was dressed in a black knit cap and long charcoal gray jacket. He handed her a longer outer coat and pointed out to leave the one she'd found upstairs on the sofa. Without a word, Mirah followed him to the garage and slid onto the soft leather seat of his car while he waited to close the passenger car door. She knew he heard the phone conversation; otherwise, why would he have been waiting on her. Having someone, even him, at that moment to be there with her was comforting. She had no idea if she'd be able to keep it together once at the police station.

Ayularc had chosen a track of symphony music in hopes of keeping Mirah's thoughts from ricocheting in her head. He could tell she was upset; who could blame her. She didn't know what had happened to her husband for some time now nor how to move on with her life. Living in limbo was not healthy for any self-aware being. Thoughts of being in The Void trickled into his mind. Not wanting to revisit them unnecessarily, he reached for Mirah's hand. A shock from her touch was more appealing than memories of The Void.

She was like ice, and no electrical current leaped out at his contact with her hand. "Why didn't you tell me you were cold? My body regulates heat a bit different than yours."

"Hmmm, oh, yeah. I guess I am a bit cold; I just didn't notice it."

Ayularc turned the heater on in the car while also engaging the heat gage for her seat. After a few minutes, she was less frigid to the touch. "I'm here if you want to talk about anything I mean."

"Hmmm, thanks. I'm just trying to imagine what the detective found out. Working to stay positive, you know?" Mirah flashed a half-smile, eyes nowhere near matching that of her upturned mouth.

"Well, whatever he has to show you, I'll be here. I do know a thing or two about relationships that transcend. All I'm saying is that you are not alone. I mean, I may not be the *usual go-to person,* but I stand by my words. You are not alone!"

They drove along in silence, allowing the music's sounds to wash away unpleasant thoughts that seemed to want their way that night. Ayularc made the forty-minute drive in twenty. Mirah hadn't noticed as she let the landscape's blur hypnotize her through the car's window. It felt as if butterflies attacked without mercy in her stomach once the car was parked and Ayularc was standing with a hand outstretched to help her out of his car.

The walk into the police station was quiet, all but for the sound of their feet slapping wet pavement. Once the automatic front door opened, the station's busyness was almost deafening to Mirah, causing her to stiffen.

Ayularc's gentle nudge in the center of her back kept her moving forward towards the front desk.

The duty sergeant was short and muscular. His uniform snug, and his hands multitasked from keyboard to passing paperwork to another officer walking by to having a caller hold the phone line.

"Can I help you, folks?"

"Yes, Mrs. Maurez here to see Detective Sykes."

"Yes, please have a seat over there. He'll be right out," the sergeant said while pointing to several short rows of chairs, all bolted to the floor.

Before Mirah had a chance to begin another mental ping-pong match of all the things which could have summoned her there, Detective Sykes rounded a corner at her right. He was a slim built man with light brown hair. His brown eyes looked tired, as if he hadn't gotten a good night's sleep in days. With a gentle smile, he greeted Mirah then Ayularc, directing them to follow him across the room and down a corridor lined with closed doors. Their walk ended outside the fifth one on the left.

Inside was a metal table with four chairs, two on each side of it. Mirah took the seat farthest from the door, as Ayularc did his best to sit next to her and blend into the room. This was her business; he was only there for support—no need for the detective to make anything to be about him.

"Mrs. Maurez, I have some information about your husband that is personal. Would you like for us to speak in private?" Detective Sykes' eyes never left her face. He wanted to be sure she would answer without any sign of manipulation. His line of work was all about the body language, and the man sitting across from him was not giving up much.

"Thank you, but please, whatever you have to say, you can say it," Mirah nodded toward Ayularc, acknowledging the detective's concerns for privacy.

"Very well, then. Mrs. Maurez, I'm sorry to have to inform you that we found your husband's body two days ago. Our department and all jurisdictions surrounding the site were notified about a local resident's report who happened to be on the road where Mr. Maurez's car was found. The person who discovered the scene had called their local sheriff's office to report burnt wreckage."

Mirah felt the air in her stomach rush out. Her head was starting to sway, then a strong arm circled her shoulders, keeping her steady. With a sudden inhaling of breath, she bit down on her lower lip, bracing for more news.

"We were able to identify his remains from DNA found. Your husband, from the evidence found and reviewed, was in a car accident. The crash occurred on a very curvy stretch of road to the north of the city, three towns over. Forensics shows that he was most likely sleepy or tired and, as a result, didn't react in time to the curved roads.

His vehicle swerved into a tree then tumbled down an embankment. The car burst into flames on the way down but wasn't discovered for some time due to the on and off rainstorms in the area. Also, the fact that the road he was driving on is not frequently used."

"Where does this road lead to?" Mirah asked, trying to figure out where Tito was going.

"It leads to an abandoned mill, then connects to an exit off Interstate 20. As I said, the road does not get traveled much. There really isn't anything out there to see. Do you have any idea why your husband would be taking that route?"

"No. We had been arguing, and things weren't going well between us for a while. I thought he'd go cool off and come back home in a few days, but..."

"I see, Mrs. Maurez. Are you able to shed some light as to where your husband may have gone to cool off whenever you'd both have an argument or disagreement?"

"Uhmm, he has family about two hundreds miles away, over in Mellcoop County. But none of them has seen him in months."

"I see. Well, he could have been taking that road to get there. Is there anything else you can tell me about his frame of mind the last time you saw him?"

The words made Mirah's mouth go dry, *the last time you saw him*. "Ahh, he was upset. Said he needed a break and was going to clear his head. I watched him get into his car from our apartment window and speed off down the street. That was the last time I saw him." Mirah's voice trailed off as the moments of the memory played before her.

"How long did the forensic evidence show Mr. Maurez as being deceased?" Ayularc asked since the detective had not specified, and Mirah was clearly not in the frame of mind to ask such a relevant question.

Detective Sykes looked at Ayularc, then back at Mirah, who stared back with questioning eyes. Taking a breath, the detective said in a low voice, "The evidence shows that the accident happened about five or so years ago. I would say the same night you saw him drive off, Mrs. Maurez. I'm sorry for your loss, and if there is anything I can do, please let me know."

"Are there any remains...I mean anything left to bury?" Mirah questioned with fresh tears splashing her lap.

"Not really. We were able to make an identification from the vehicle and very little remnants of DNA inside the car. I'm sorry, Mrs. Maurez," Detective Sykes said, closing the file folder in front of him as he pushed a piece of paper and a pen towards her. "I just need your signature next to the X to certify that you have been informed of the evidence found in this case."

With a nod, Mirah grabbed the pen and did her best to sign the paper. Her signature went uphill as she struggled to write straight along the line. Once she was done, she pushed the pen and paper back towards the detective, who then stood and somberly said,

"If you need a moment, please feel free to remain here. You can leave whenever you're ready. Again, I am sorry for your loss, Mrs. Maurez." With a nod to them both, the detective left the room, gently closing the door behind him. The room suddenly felt cold, like a tomb to Mirah. The feeling of sadness and death permeated from the dull grey-blue walls.

Ayularc said nothing; he only continued to hold Mirah's shoulders, reminding her she wasn't alone. They remained in the room for a few moments before she finally spoke.

"Take me home, please." It was almost a whisper.

Without a word, Ayularc helped her out of the room and down the hall. The sounds of the precinct hurt both their ears after the cocoon effect the small room had provided. With swift feet, Ayularc ushered Mirah to his car. The warmth and comforting smell of the leather seats allowed her body to relax finally.

As the car drove out of the parking lot, she stared without focus on the road ahead. "He'd been dead all this time," she softly said. All this time, I thought he'd just left me. Abandoned our marriage, even though I felt it couldn't be, still most of me had come to believe this." She began to whimper as guilt tried to consume her. "I should have stopped him. If I did, he'd still be here and..."

"Stop it! You, nor anyone else, holds your future. You had a disagreement. Things weren't going well between you both, and no matter what you convince yourself of, it takes two working hard together to make a relationship work. You can not spend the next five years of your life blaming yourself, Mirah. You must find a way to let go of this guilt and blame so you can move on. So you can live."

Mirah said nothing; instead, she listened to Ayularc's words and prayed quietly inside her mind for peace. She had done her grieving the second year Tito didn't come home. She knew then it was over because he didn't even bother to collect any of his things from their apartment and never had any money been withdrawn from their joint bank accounts.

Then there were the dreams. Dreams that he was cut off from her. She just assumed they meant their relationship was over, not that he was dead. The few tears she had left continued to fall, but they were tears now of regret. Sadness that they'd never been able to get past the things which now seemed petty and small. They were from different worlds, she and Tito, but that was the attraction in the beginning. Still, attraction alone, they'd both realized, was not enough for a lasting marriage.

She said to take her home, but we both know that's not a good idea right now. Could she have meant my home? Well, it doesn't matter because my home is the only one she'll know for some time to come.

The sleek sedan was parked in its space inside Ayularc's garage. Mirah fumbled with the door handle only to have her companion open it from the outside before she could figure out how to make it comply.

"Would you like some tea or a snack? I could sure use something."

"Yes, some tea sounds lovely, but I'm not really sure my stomach can take food right now."

“Understood. I’ll meet you in the living room then,” Ayularc said with a quick raise of his eyebrows in hopes of lightening the mood. Mirah smiled briefly and then made her way to the living room, curling up on the long sofa.

By the time Ayularc arrived with a laden tray, she was fast asleep. He chuckled to himself and set the tray down, eating his snack as he watched her rest. The wind had picked up since they arrived back at the house, and his gaze went to the still closed blinds. Its low howl reminded him of Humtracks and their numbers, which soon would be on the hunt for blood. Rh-negative blood—Mirah’s blood.

CHAPTER 18

Once he'd finished his tea and snack, Ayularc had helped Mirah up the stairs and to her room. After she was comfortably tucked under the blanket, he went to his own bedroom and ready for bed. Being around her those past several hours had his core temperature high. He needed to cool down and opted to sleep bare. The coolness in his room brought slow relief from the heat's discomfort. He needed to control his humanity. Mirah was becoming harder to be around; even with all his mind had to juggle, she was the most challenging of puzzles. *It's going to be a long night...ahhh!*

As he tried to sleep, thoughts of his encounters with Mirah through her dreams circled him. He found them sweet and tempting. She was like forbidden nectar, and parts of him were parched from his long existence. He was experiencing The Rage. That's what The Fathers called the raging heat that consumed their bodies once they'd decided to take human women. They had no idea the same would affect their offspring, not all but a percentage of those created when their father and human mother joined. The sentiments of his father echoed in his ears of how he was his most beloved child. *My father was going through The Rage because of my mother. He loved her! I can not imagine how he felt when he understood I would be the end of her. My birth would be one she would not survive. Could that be the reason I am the last he has seeded all this time?*

Ayularc's thoughts then drifted to the sleeping wonder in the room down the hall. She deserved as wonderful a life as any, but he was biased. Mirah was special, unique, and her life, he would do all he could to protect. If his kind had any evidence of her existence, he knew it would be him racing against time—and time was merciless.

Still, were his feelings for Basielle or Mirah? They were joined for a long time, and how could he be sure which pulled at him. *Simple, the one who has no ulterior motive.* Basielle's motives were easy for him to see. But what of Mirah's? What was the reason she followed his instructions without much hesitation? She was powerful, and he felt she knew it too. Why else would she pray so much and fast if it weren't to build up her spiritual powers? But this pull was new, fresh. What he shared with Basielle was intense, but it was also like tug-a-war. Her lust for power was constant, and if she could have it all without him, Ayularc knew she'd take that chance.

"No!" He said out loud as if to quiet the debate between his mind and spirit. "No, it is not her. Basielle only remained by my side because of the territory I worked to gain. There were others more handsome and stronger than I once was. It was my skillfulness in many areas of life that she valued, or I should say, hoped to control. Still, I am not like The Fathers; I am Nephilim, half-human, and that part of my spirit will fight for her, for me, for whatever twisted existence The Most High will allow me to live."

The mental banter continued for Ayularc well into the morning. It wasn't until after 3:00 AM he finally succumbed to sleepful bliss. He dreamt of nothing for a while, then he saw her. Mirah was standing with her back towards him. She was having a conversation, no an argument with someone he couldn't quite see. There were no audible words, but he could see from her body movements and hand gestures things were getting heated. He moved closer, and just before he was able to almost reach out and touch Mirah, she moved her body a step to the left. Black hair danced on unseen wind. A face like he'd never seen before now scowled at Mirah. Even for him, it gave a fright, but Mirah stood her ground, not moved by the grotesqueness staring back at her.

Neither of them noticed him as he circled them, trying to read their lips, straining his ears to hear what they were saying—nothing. Then he touched an arm; in an instant, Basielle turned to him, face looking as he remembered, no longer grotesque. She called his name, and he gasped. *She can see me?*

"Yu Elle? Yu Elle, my love. At last, I've found you. How are you here? I've tried for so long to reach you?"

Unable to think of what to say, Ayularc let go of Basielle's arm. Instantly the moment was gone, and she returned her focus on Mirah as if Ayularc had never interrupted. To test his theory, he touched her arm again. Just as before, she turned to him, questioning again how it was he was there.

So I can speak to her, here in Mirah's dreams—interesting! This will be useful in the days ahead. I have to question Mirah when she wakes on what this argument was all about.

"Basielle," Ayularc called as he touched her arm once more. "I think I've found a way to free you, For you to walk among men again."

"I knew you would, Yu Elle. I knew you'd find a way as long as I could reach you."

"Of course, my love. I just need you to be gentle with this human's body. I need it to be unharmed in order to free you. Do you understand?"

"Yes, my love. I will do all to protect it from harm. But hurry, my love. I don't know how much longer I can hold onto this realm. I feel myself slipping back there. I don't want to go back there. Hurry, Yu Elle. HURRY!"

Ayularc snatched his hand back so forcefully, he woke from his sleep. Sun rays were kissing the lower edges of the windows, and he could hear Mirah groaning in her sleep. *She's still dreaming.*

A bouquet of beautiful mixed flowers greeted Mirah when she came out of the bathroom that morning. She hadn't heard anyone enter the bedroom, but that didn't surprise her at all. Everyone but her in the house had the uncanny ability to move silently. She swore that they only did the occasional sound effects of footsteps and throat clearing so she'd not be startled. From the cleanliness of the place, she knew someone or thing kept it spotless. Mirah wasn't sure if the cook did it all, but nothing in that place would be a surprise.

The living room was empty, but sounds floated down from the dining area on the second floor. She rounded the corner and took the stairs to be greeted by a sun-filled space and a savory breakfast spread. Ayularc was ending a phone call when she took a seat at the table. As usual, it was just the two of them, though she could sense someone else nearby, somewhere in the house. She presumed it to be the cook, who always made something she favored. Mirah thought for sure it was all Ayularc's doing. He was a great host, always sure her needs were met and eating whatever he thought would please her most.

"Good morning, and thank you so much for the flowers. They are beautiful and fill my room with sweet perfume," Mirah beamed. The thought had lifted her spirits, especially after last night. "Also, thanks for coming with me last night and getting me to bed. I barely remember anything once I sat on the sofa."

"One, you're most welcome, and two, sat was not actually what you did on the sofa. It was more like curled up in a ball and passed out."

They both chuckled for a moment at the thought of her passed out on the sofa, instead of being awake, waiting on him to bring the tea. Her laughter moved Ayularc; even with all the endless blows life was hitting her with, she could still laugh—genuinely laugh. She turned again to look out toward the sunrise. The sky was sunny, even though there were looming grey clouds. The fresh air coming off the bay filled her lungs as she took in a deep cleansing breath.

"So, how did you sleep."

Without turning her head from the view and with eyes now focused on a boat heading out to sea, she replied, "It was a little restless, but then you know this already. I can tell you have a question; just ask."

Ayularc liked that Mirah was not one for much small talk. Her directness caused the corners of his mouth to bend upward briefly.

"Very well. What were you and Basielle arguing about?"

Mirah turned her gaze to look at Ayularc just in time to see him take a bite of his jam covered toast with a deep sigh. "She wanted me to release the hold I've been able to maintain over her lately. It limits her ability to take over a lot of my subconscious. To tell you the truth, I had no idea that was happening. It was only after prayer this morning The Most High told me it's because of the fasting and praying for release from bloodline covenants that I'm able to do so. Still, I'm not completely free from her. I guess I have a lot more spiritual warfare yet to do. You talking to her, that was new? Did you have any idea you could do that?"

"No, I didn't know. I just touched her and saw the effect it had. It certainly helps, though."

"Oh, how so?" Mirah questioned, now digging into her breakfast.

"Well, I can tell her what I need from her. What I need her to do, in order to separate both of your spirits."

"And the side effects, to me in particular?"

"None that I'm aware of. But, I need you to pray and fast more. My plan should be ready to unfold any day now."

"Hmmm, I guess my options are few, and if it will get the target off my back your kind placed there, I'm willing to try it. Will you at least give me some specifics of your scheme?"

"The less you know, the better. I can't afford for Basielle to get wind of any details."

"But she was, *is* your wife. Why does she knowing anything matter?"

"The Basielle I was married to, believe me, this world can do without. I miss the companionship, yes, but our marriage was to serve her more than me. I see it as fate that we are not together now, and I don't plan to tamper with fate."

Master, I've found the human female that would be more than suitable for your needs, Flyenz interrupted.

Good. We're having breakfast right now. I can entertain Mirah for another hour if that's all the time you need to put her in my lab.

No need, I'm outside, and the female is unconscious as requested. I will be in and out of the house in less than ten.

Good. How long before the subject wakes?

The dose I gave her should wear off in about an hour. Should I stay with her until then?

Yes, thanks, Flyenz. I'll be there before she wakes. It looks like today is the day to execute my plan.

"And just like that, fate answers your question," Ayularc said with a smile to Mirah.

"What do you mean?" She mumbled as she worked on her last piece of toast.

"Well, it would seem that today, my plan to help you be free of Basielle goes into motion. Eat up; you're going to need your strength. I know I will."

Not wanting to push further, Mirah ate her breakfast, grabbing a second helping of fruit. *Father, whatever this is, he's got planned, keep me covered. I know you have a purpose for my life, and Ayularc's involvement in it is not by chance. I trust you, Father; you alone.*

Once they were both stuffed, Ayularc rose from the table and told Mirah to follow him. They descended the stairs, and instead of turning to go towards the living room, they took the hallway heading towards the garage. Before Mirah could tell him to wait for her to get her bag, thinking they were going out, he stopped, touched a spot on the wall, and an opening appeared below his hand.

Mirah gasped in surprise and slowly followed Ayularc inside. Laying on a metal table was a rather tall, beautiful woman. She was sleeping, at least Mirah hoped she was. Her clothing was that of a pair of jeans, a cotton long sleeve blouse, and red heels on her feet. She wore little makeup—a natural beauty. Sitting near the table on a metal stool was a man dressed in all black. He had greasy looking hair slicked back, and intense slant eyes which remained focused on the woman stretched out before him.

"Mirah, this is Flyenz. He is a trusted associate of mine."

"Hello," Mirah said in a quiet voice, not wanting to disturb the sleeping woman.

Flyenz only nodded toward Mirah, momentarily finding her gaze before returning it to the woman who was slowly starting to come out of the induced sleep.

"I'm sure you have questions, Mirah, but I must ask that you keep quiet while I prep our volunteer here. Alright?"

Mirah just nodded her head and took a seat on another metal stool just off to her left. She let her eyes take in the room and all its contents. It was definitely a lab of sorts. Medical equipment lined the walls on tables, a few free-standing in place. Shelves, too, lined with vials and jars filled with only God knows. If she hadn't known better, she'd think it was a lab at any research facility, but this was all in a private residence, far away from neighbors, owned by a Nephilim. *What's there to be concerned about!* With a deep breath, she pushed back her nerves and focused on being rid of Basielle. That thought alone calmed her considerably.

"Hello there! It's okay; you are all right and safe. No one here is going to harm you. My name is Ayularc, and my associates here would like to offer you a proposition of sorts."

The woman eyed them all, fear evident in her eyes until she saw Mirah. Something about the tenderness of her face made her relax a little.

"Wha, what happened to me? How did I get here?"

"Well, I can explain. You see, I needed someone with your uniqueness to take part in something like an acting job."

"But I'm not an actress," the woman said, voice still laced with fear as her eyes darted between Ayularc and Mirah, not daring to look at Flyenz, who had now moved to the farthest corner of the room.

"Well, that's the beauty of it all. You don't have to do much acting, and there won't be any cameras rolling, so you won't get camera shy. You see, I need someone to just say a few words to my friend Mirah here. Mirah, say hello," Ayularc coaxed, not waiting for Mirah to speak. "Anyways, it's all quite simple, really. Kind of like a sleep study. You see, Mirah here has a hard time sleeping, and I'm trying to get to the bottom of what is causing it on a subconscious level."

The woman gazed back at Mirah, still with questioning looks on her face, not sure if she believed the tale Ayularc was spinning.

"But why me? What makes me qualified to help out? Shouldn't this be done with medical professionals? Which I'm not, by the way."

"Good point, but you just happen to look most like Mirah's mother when she was younger. I do believe that the event which started her issues was from an earlier period in her life. Look, I've planned to make it very worth your while financially, say to the tune of one hundred thousand—cash of course."

The woman's eyes widened. That kind of money would set her up nicely. She could pay off most of her debt and finally move out of the city. "Well, what exactly do you need me to do? And how long do I have to stay here?"

"I have a script all printed out here for you to say when I give you the signal, and if all goes as hoped, Flyenz here will take you home tonight. How does that sound?"

“Hmmm, alright, but I want to see the money. Upfront!”

“Of course.” Ayularc reached for a small black bag under the desk next to him, unzipping it, pulling the sides apart. He let the woman look at its contents. Straps of US Currency in mixed denominations stared back at her. She grabbed a few straps and fanned the bills, making sure they were full of bills and not just paper. Satisfied, she nodded to Ayularc. “Good. Oh, where are my manners? Would you care for something to eat? Drink?”

“Something to eat and drink would be nice, thanks,” the woman said; still a little hesitant, shaking her head while widening her eyes, attempting to wake more from the drugged sleep.

As if on cue, Ayularc’s cook appeared at the opening of the room. He set the tray on the desk next to Ayularc, who then helped the woman down from the table so she could sit at his desk and eat.

Mirah watched it all, still confused as to what Ayularc was up to. Flyenz unnerved her, and Ayularc sensed it. In an attempt to get rid of the room's heaviness, Ayularc engaged the woman in small talk about her life. How she’d come to live in the city and if she had any plans for the money she was about to earn.

Mirah took the opportunity to pray. She closed her eyes and blocked out the rest of the energy flying off the others in the room. She needed to center herself. It was about to be a long day.

CHAPTER 19

Boss's phone number glared on the cell phone's screen. After two rings, a fat finger pressed the button to accept the call. The man swallowed hard, knowing he couldn't avoid this moment any longer.

"Yes, Boss?"

"It's been a long minute since I received any updates from you. What's the latest?

"Ahh, nothing actually. She hasn't returned to her apartment since yesterday, and the laptop has not been turned on either. I've even put permanent eyes on her place as of this morning, in case she does a drive-by or visits with one of her neighbors. It's like she disappeared."

"She came back yesterday, and you didn't have her followed?! " The man grimaced, wanting to kick something for not having one of his guys stay to stake out the place. The truth was, he was on a tight budget and figured the woman would turn on her laptop, exposing her location once she'd left the apartment. He'd hope to save the extra cash, not having to pay one of the men. "What about friends, coworkers?"

"My guys report nothing. She hasn't made any physical contact with the shortlist of people she associates with."

A gruff sound came from the phone as the man bit down on his thumb at what he hoped wouldn't come next.

"Listen, I don't care if you have to go door to door in the city, FIND HER! You've got forty-eight hours before I make another arrangement. Arrangements that will prove your services are no longer a viable option. Understand?"

"You got it, Boss. I'll get on it right away; no need to do anything hasty. Forty-eight hour, got it."

"Hasty? Hasty would have been me, severing ties with you after the first day. I mean it, you've got forty-eight hours before I resort to more unnatural methods."

"Yes, Bo..." The phone call ended before the man could finish. He stared at the now black screen of his cell phone. His reflection showed furrowed eyebrows as he thought of how to finish the hide and seek job. He'd need to call for reinforcements, which meant more money out of his cut. *Better to lose money than my head!*

After exhaling a deep sigh, he flipped through his contacts and dialed the number for Lawrence. Law, as he was known on the streets, was in charge of a large crew over on the east side of the city. He had people into almost everything and eyes not only on his territory but also that of neighboring ones. Because he owned the docks, he controlled the lifeline of imports into the area. Everyone knows that in order to eat in this city, Law has to get his cut.

"It's been a long time. You must really be hurting if you're calling me," Law said on answering the call.

"Hey, Law. Yeah, well, this is something that has to get done. A lot on the line, and let's just say, the client takes *satisfaction guaranteed* literally."

"Hmmm, so what can I do for you?"

"I need your eyes and ears. Missing female needing to be found. Just need a location, that's all."

"A female? It must be someone serious or very threatening for you to come to me. What time frame am I looking at?"

"Thirty-six hours tops."

"Which means your absolute deadline is forty-eight. Fine. Send me whatever intel you have, and I'll get my people on it right away, as soon as I get confirmation of my deposit, of course. The bank account number is still the same. Wait, your client wouldn't happen to be connected to the Rizeen Towers project, would they?"

"The Rizeen Towers, what makes you think that?"

"Word is, there is a team of heavy hitters looking to scoop that project. Thing is though, nobody has laid eyes on who they are. Speculation is they're from out of town, international, old-world money."

"Hmmm, don't know about any connection to Rizeen Towers. All I will say is, they aren't the type you ask questions of. You take directives, execute, and deliver on time."

Sounds like I need an introduction. "Tell you what, I'm gonna make you a unique offer. I'll find your girl, IF she's still in this city. Won't even charge the usual fee for such a rushed job. I'll do it in exchange for an introduction to your client. An in-person introduction."

"Hmmm, I don't know if that's possible. They aren't the type to be contacted. They're the ones that contact you."

"All the same. You let them know I'll be the one bringing the whereabouts of your missing girl and will only give up the goods in person. Don't sweat; I'll be sure to let them know it was all your wisdom that reached out and added me to your search team. What do you say?"

A fat hand rubbed the three-day-old beard of the man's face. *Nothing to lose and no money lost on this deal. Hell, I'll just be glad to have this wrapped up as quickly as possible, with my reputation and head intact. Who knows, this might be my way out. Law could take my place, and what's making all this money good for if I'm dead?* "Sounds like you've got a deal, Law. I'll text you her photo and information now. You get me confirmation you have the details of her location, and I'll get you that introduction."

"Done! I'll be seeing you in thirty-six."

Law leaned back in the dark brown rawhide leather desk chair. A broad grin stretched across his face as he let his gaze lose focus, looking at the office ceiling. He was well aware of the hidden powers moving in the shadows of the city. His spiritists had explained several of the dreams he'd had over the past few years. Dreams that indicated power, old power was coming to change the area's financial flow and control the landscape. A landscape he planned to maintain his hands on. He'd just been biding his time to make a move. In less than thirty-six hours, he'd intended to be sitting at the table when power in the city was being redistributed.

⌘⌘⌘⌘⌘⌘

“Okay, my dear. I need you to lay back down on the table and try to relax, alright?” Ayularc coaxed in as light a voice as he could manage. His extra big smile helped to put the woman at ease, just a little.

Within about five minutes, she struggled to keep her eyes open. Once she was totally relaxed, Flyenz brought a metal stool next to her side again. Sitting on it, he intently watched for any sudden changes in her movements.

Mirah looked from the woman, now relaxed on the metal table, to Ayularc, questioning with her eyes what was going to happen next. Seeing her expression, Ayularc obliged her with an explanation.

“Basically, while our subject here is in an induced relaxed state, I will use the newly learned information about how to communicate with Basielle and have her make a covenant with the subject. All going according to plan, she will leave your body and bind with this one,” Ayularc stated, raising his eyebrows and shoulders as he did.

“Okay, but I’m wide awake.”

“Yes, about that. I’m going to need to drug you.”

“Excuse you?”

"Don't worry; you will be fine. The effects will wear off in an hour or so."

Mirah looked at him wearily. She was not fond of the idea of being drugged and still had apprehensions about Ayularc's grand vision of freeing her of Basielle's spirit. But she'd prayed and told The Father she'd trust his plan for her life. So, now she needed to put her words into action. *Okay, Father, let your will be done.*

Mirah took a seat at the desk. Taking the tiny pill handed to her, she washed it down with water from an extra glass on Ayularc's desk. She felt the effects almost immediately, letting her head fall back and rest on the headrest of the desk chair. Soon her vision of the lab was replaced with one again of the field of flowers in the place Ayularc had called The Grove. This time the sun was not so bright, and the colors of the flowers appeared dull. She found little pleasure there now as before.

As she began to become restless, the familiar image of a black-haired beauty approached just off in the distance. It moved in a jerking motion, not fluid as she was accustomed to seeing it glide over surfaces. Her face, though now seemed to lack its fullness. The skin of her cheeks were pulled taught as if she were starving, but here, no one ate food. At least not the kind that was chewed and digested in the stomach.

Ayularc appeared just off to her left, waiting with her for Basielle to approach. When she was close enough to touch, he placed a hand on her arm, pulling it toward him instead of Mirah.

"Basielle. Basielle, it's me."

"Yu Elle? Yu Elle, is it really you, or am I imagining you here?"

"Yes, my love. It's me. I've come to free you from this confining place. Wouldn't you like that?"

"Freedom! Yes, I want to be free. I want to be in complete control again. Oh, please, my love, set me free!"

"Yes, *yes*. That's why I'm here, but in order for you to be free, you'll have to do exactly as I say, alright?"

"Yes, anything. Just get me out of this prison!" Basielle's full attention was locked onto Ayularc. She hadn't noticed that Mirah had taken several steps back, just out of her reach.

"Okay, Basielle. I've procured a flesh suit for you. One that by human standards is beautiful, still incomparable to your beauty, of course. It is young-looking and fit. A great host for you to control at will. All that is needed is for you to release your covenant with Mirah and her bloodline and take that of the bloodline flowing in your new flesh suit."

"That's it? Shouldn't she be here? I can't sense anyone else."

"It is a bit different than the process you did with Mirah's ancestor. The body is physically in my home, my love, and in a relaxed state. All that is needed are the words spoken by you, to break the old covenant with Mirah and form a new one with your host, Leah. That's it. That's all you have to do, my love. My beautiful Basielle."

"How long will I be able to use her body before needing a new one?"

"Many years for sure. Before that time comes, though, we will have created you a new flesh suit made to withstand the power of your spirit better."

"But none of my original DNA was found. How can you make a flesh suit for me?"

"A lot of progress has been made in the process, my dear. I have been conducting my own personal research using Rh-negative blood and its donors' DNA to help formulate a base to which some of my own DNA is added. This is to make for a stable environment which would be compatible for any of those still roaming The Void to bind with." Ayularc sounded so convincing that even Mirah looked impressed. She didn't recall him admitting any of this in his plan, nor the name of the woman laid out in the lab.

"I knew you'd find a way. You are even more brilliant than before, Yu Elle. I chose wisely when we mated.

Yes, you did, and I fell for your beauty and charms. How gullible I was, but that was many lifetimes ago.

Mirah stiffened when they both looked at her in unison. Suddenly they moved as one toward her, but she remained planted. She accepted Ayularc's outstretched hand, which he placed into Basielle's.

"Now, Basielle, for the first step. Break the covenant between you and Mirah's bloodline."

Hesitantly, Basielle looked from Mirah to Ayularc then back to Mirah again. After a moment of mental checking, she spoke the words needed to break the covenant formed many lifetimes ago by Mirah's ancestor.

Mirah felt a pulling in her stomach as if something she had eaten wanted out. Muscles in her back joined in, contracting violently, causing her to bend at the waist, then drop to one knee. Black, oily liquid spewed from her mouth, onto flowers at her feet. Upon contact with the fluid, the flowers dissolved as if acid was being poured on them. Mirah gagged, heaved, then spewed the rancid liquid again. Even in this dream state, she could smell its foul odor.

Black and foul, just like her spirit, Ayularc thought as he watched every trace of Basielle's spirit manifest as it left Mirah's body. *Good, get it all out, every piece of her,* he thought as if Mirah could hear him. She looked up and locked eyes with him at that moment as if she had.

Mirah didn't realize that in the lab, her physical body mirrored the motions as in the dream. Flyenz was holding her hair away from her face as her body leaned forward and she dry heaved into a small trash can.

When it was all out, the black liquid slid along the ground toward Basielle, withered flowers in its wake. Upon contact with her foot, it absorbed into her. Ayularc motioned for Mirah to step back further. He didn't want her to remain so close to Basielle now, should something not go according to his plan.

"Now, my love, call out to Leah. Offer her wealth beyond reason; this I've found to be a weakness of hers, one you can easily exploit. Give her the promise of generational wealth if she joins you in a covenant."

"But I can't see her; there is nothing here to link me to her in the physical realm."

"Here," Ayularc handed Basielle a lock of Leah's hair. Somehow he'd gotten it before arriving after Mirah had passed out. Being a Nephilim, he was able to pass through realms and easily bring things with him too.

"Yes, she has lovely hair. Her body will do nicely," Basielle cooed as she grasped the lock of hair and began to call out to Leah.

Mirah watched, now unable to hear the words Basielle spoke. She sensed no one else there but Ayularc, and as moments passed, the vision of Basielle faded. Nothing remained that linked the women together, but how was it that she could still see Ayularc? He saw her questioning gaze, and for a moment, sadness covered his face. He understood the dangerous truth—he was the link. His humanity had become desirous of her, all the time they'd spent together, his dreams she invaded. All had created a connection between them. They were now in a covenant, even if she didn't realize it.

CHAPTER 20

A shockwave went through The Fathers. Each felt it where they stood. It felt as if something momentarily drained them of energy, and painfully so. The only sound that could be heard was that of Humtracks being corralled in their pens. Lu finally stood up straight, eyes ablaze like hot branding irons. Nothing needed to be said among them; they knew something spiritual, something from The Light, had caused this new sensation, this new discomfort.

Momentarily, the general assigned to finding the human link appeared on one knee before Lu. He could barely stop from shaking as he knew inevitable wrath would be his because he replies to the question rolling towards Lu's mouth.

"Where is this human! Why hasn't their location been given to me?"

"I have people combing the city for her. She has not been seen in days."

"Combing the city? COMBING THE CITY!!! THEN USE A BRUSH AND FIND HER!!!" Lu's voice rumbled in the space with such force that all nearby had to steady themselves so as not to topple over. "You and your band of humans have one cycle of the sun to bring here location to me," Lu growled, now stooping low enough for only the cowering general to hear. "If you don't have what I want, I will take matters into my own hands. Prepare to offer your sacrifice should you fail," Lu continued, his eyes still glowing like red hot irons, but his face appearing not as one of exquisite beauty but like that of a deformed melted mask.

Without another word, the general rose and dashed off. Once he was some distance away from Lu, he checked in with his spies, who informed him that they were working double-time to find the female. He assured them that if they didn't deliver, none would see the noonday sun.

⌘⌘⌘⌘⌘⌘

What did you do?!

Not now, father.

Yes, now! Lu is on the warpath and felt, hell, we all felt a shift in the realm. It was powerful and from The Light. I know you have something to do with it, you and whatever it is you've got planned there!

I'm a bit busy father fixing this mess. I will reach out soon, but please, I have to go!

You better, because by sunrise tomorrow, Lu is taking the search into his own hands.

Sunrise?

Yes, SUNRISE!

CHAPTER 21

Something lingered. Lu smacked his lips as if tasting the air. He replayed the event in his mind; he felt something familiar on the fringes of the pain; specs of darkness that he just couldn't place. His eyes scanned around him. Everyone was busy with their tasks, preparing for Humtrack laden ships' next wave soon to be deployed. None seemed to be still focused on the disturbing event as he was. Even so, he knew if they were, they'd not willfully show it.

His mind focused again on the specs of darkness. It was like something just out of reach in his memory. He knew it, just couldn't recall what it was. *What is it?*

"Lu," another general called his name, slamming his mind's door to memories, shut with unexpected force. He turned, trying to hide his annoyance. "Another litter of Humtracks was born, and four litters are prepped, ready to hunt."

"At last, some good news. Perfect. See that they are assigned to ships and have everyone on standby to deploy at sunrise. Regardless of what I find out, we escalate our matters. We still have many in The Void who need flesh suits and reclaim the earth. See that the labs are ready to receive the new harvest of DNA."

"Consider it done!"

⌘⌘⌘⌘⌘⌘

Ayularc had taken Mirah to her room to sleep off the remaining effects of the medication he'd given her earlier. Flyenz was following his instructions and had taken Leah, in his car, back towards the city. She was still out of it, and based on the dosage she'd received to keep her sedated, she'd be out for at least another four hours.

It was just approaching 2:00 PM as Flyenz took a back road instead of the highway that led straight into the heart of the city. Leah was too perfect for this role. She was living alone and had no close relatives in the area. A transplant from down South, she'd come to the city like many, to break free and be independent. But the city could be a dangerous place to stretch one's wings. The years he'd spent with Ayularc had prepared him to do many of the most unthinkable things, but he was happy to do it. Ayularc had saved him from The Void, and when no one would give him a place in their territory, Ayularc welcomed him without question. Anything he could want was his. Truthfully, he didn't want much. He just wanted never to return to The Void, and if being at Ayularc's beck and call secured him from such a fate, he was all in.

The set of warehouses came into view as his car rounded a curve; the sign could be seen from there; Blue Light Trucking. The place was lifeless since there was nothing scheduled for the trucks, and the creation of a body for Basielle was put on permanent hold. He punched the passcode into the gate's security panel and waited for it to roll open. Once inside the property, he drove around to the last loading bay, which was lower than those designed for trucks.

Every movement he made echoed in the open space. He walked over toward a panel just to the right of his car. After pressing the on a button, he looked back at Leah, still passed out in the front seat of this car. A buzzy sound came from the panel as he pressed, and a light above his finger turned green.

Without a second thought, he opened the passenger side car door and scooped Leah into his arms. Propping her up against the side of his car, he took one last look at the beautiful face before him, her head being held steady by his strong hand. His face remained emotionless; with one blink of his eyes and quick motion, he snapped her neck. The sound caused a nearby bird to flutter away. Leah's lifeless body was hoisted over Flyenz's shoulder as he spun around and pulled an orange lever on the steel door next to the wall panel with the glowing bright green button. The heat from the furnace licked the air around him. Waves of heat danced towards him, warming his face as he leaned slightly forward. One shift of Leah's body off his shoulder caused it to tumble down the shoot into the hungry roaring red, yellow, and orange flames.

Flynez took a step back but kept the furnaces' door open to witness the body burn. Once it was engulfed in flames, he closed the door and climbed onto the hood of his car, stretching to full length. With fingers laced behind his head, he closed his eyes and listened to the sounds of the afternoon both inside the loading bay and the area around the warehouse. After about three hours, he opened the furnace door and saw that Leah's body had completely burned.

Master, it's done.

Thank you, Flyenz.

I will need you to stay at the house starting tonight. I expect we may soon have company.

As you wish. What of the burnt ashes?

Leave them there. They are of no use to anyone now.

Very well. I shall be there shortly.

⌘⌘⌘⌘⌘⌘

Ayularc's father was keeping busy working on mapping out the area assigned to him. He was meticulous. Something Lu liked dearly about him. He had been instrumental in the planning of Humtrack hunts, and though he had paid in the past dearly for allowing humanity to scar him, he remained loyal to the cause of The Fathers. Lu approached him in full stride, wanting to know if the latest logistics for the Humtracks had been completed. He needed something to put into motion at sunrise.

As he neared, Lu's stride began to slow. He licked his lips, and there, *right there* was the trace like that of the specs he'd felt during the event. *You, one of your offspring is the weak link!* Not wanting to play his hand too quickly, Lu proceeded to advance, trying to keep his tone level when he finally spoke.

"Do you have a route that those deployed at sunrise can use?"

"Ahh, yes. Several, in fact. Any particular area you want them deployed?"

"I have two at the moment, maybe a third."

"Okay."

"Yes, well, I'd like one focused on the city center of Vanquale and another over by its East Bay."

Ayularc's father didn't falter one inch. He knew that Lu was onto his son. The locations he chose were no coincidence and indeed not random. "Not a problem, I have just what you need."

"Perfect! I knew you would. Oh, yes, isn't that area governed by one of yours?"

"It is. Ayularc."

"Yes, Ayularc. Savior of those in The Void. Bright and very smart, just like his father. You must be so proud of him?" Lu prodded, trying to get a reaction, anything from his fallen brother before him. But after a few lingering seconds, Lu knew it was pointless. His brother would give nothing away, especially after having to lose the offspring's mother at childbirth. A birth he'd never planned to let be conceived. No, for his brother, that human woman was not to suffer the fate of so many others. She was to remain his consort, never to be tainted by their seed. "See that the information is passed on to the generals commanding the ships by later tonight."

"As you wish, Lu." Ayularc's father turned back to the electronic map before him. His focus no longer on the lines and dots but that of his son and the precious hours he had remaining.

⌘⌘⌘⌘⌘⌘

Ayularc! AYULARC!

No need to shout, father.

Time's up. At sunrise, a ship of Humtracks will be sent to the city center and another to scour the East Bay. Lu knows. I don't know how, but he knows it's you. And from the smirk he tried to hide just now, he knows the woman would most likely not be that far from wherever you are.

Hmmm, as I suspected. I believe sunrise will be more illuminating than either of us expects. Anything else you can share?

Well, he told me to have the deployment routes in the hands of the generals leading the mission by later today.

Sunrise, hmmm that strategically makes no sense. If he has you passing the route information over later today, that could only mean he intends to strike at...

MIDNIGHT! They both mentally shouted in unison.

Ayularc, what are you going to do? You can't take on that many Humtracks and generals alone?

No need to worry, father. I will do what needs to be done, as always. I've got to go. There are some things

I still need to take care of before midnight. But know that I won't make it easy on them.

Ayularc!

It'll be alright father. I have something Lu will want more than banishing me to The Void. We both know, stroking his ego is the way to staying one step ahead of him.

CHAPTER 22

Ayularc paced his lab, hands clasped behind his back, footsteps echoing in the space. His mind was sorting, categorizing information and memories faster than a supercomputer. Mirah was still upstairs, sleeping off the effects of the pill she'd taken to help her dream. He was happy, a little shocked even, that his plan worked. Basielle was successfully unlinked from Mirah, and her spirit was back in The Void. He knew she'd try again to break free, but the time it would most likely take her was more than enough for Mirah, at least to live a long and fulfilled life. *That's if Lu would let her.* His mind paused at the thought of Leah, she paid the dearest price so far for his scheme, but someone else had to. Time was starting to squeeze its claws around all of them. He had to be ready before its razor-sharp edges drew blood.

Now there were only hours left before they'd have to confront Lu's wrath or shadow of mercy. Neither would be pleasant, and he had no idea what Mirah's life would become if Lu had his way. All he was sure of was the fact that she would be, like him, an instrumental part of his kind's plan to reclaim the earth. If she could reach Nephilim, cross into their realm, Lu would stop at nothing to discover if there were other humans who could do the same. She would be emotionally and physically dissected. Though she was strong, he knew she'd not survive. How would *he* survive knowing what would be done to her? Much he'd witnessed first hand, participated in. He helped create a lot of the procedures! *No, I won't do that to her, won't let it be done either. There has to be a way around this. HAS TO BE!*

Flyenz appeared then, standing in the hallway next to the lab's opening. He waited for the storm in Ayularc's mind to settle before moving. The weight of the developing situation permeated off of Ayularc, enough so that he could feel the heaviness of dread with his current proximity.

Should I get reinforcements, Master? Fylenz asked, not wanting to speak out loud in the event Mirah was awake, wandering downstairs.

No. Any show of force will only make matters worse. Lu would see it as me having something to hide or even to protect. We go about the day as usual. Have the chef prepare an early dinner. I'll need you to be the first line of defense. Don't try to take them all on; just delay them as long as possible so that I can help Mirah.

As you wish, Master, Flyenz said before walking away.

Ayularc paced the lab for a few more minutes, then left and went to the living room. He looked out over the bay and opened one of the glass window panels, walking out onto the terrace. The day was nice and sunny, even though the strange clouds still hung in the sky. He knew they were just waiting for orders before revealing their true nature. But none of them were sent for him or Mirah. No, what would arrive for them, would not be so easily seen.

Thoughts of the conversation he'd had with his father replayed now, as a gentle breeze kissed his cheek. He closed his eyes and recalled the warning of not letting his humanity, the human side of him, overrule the plans his kind has been working on. Plans that must come to fruition if they were to survive and reclaim what was lost during The Flood. They all knew their time was limited. How much of it that still remained was uncertain. That's why the takeover was being pushed up, why spiritual activity had increased tremendously across the earth.

He took a seat on one of the nearby lounge chairs. His thoughts shifted to nothingness, and he allowed himself to sleep, just for a moment. Blue skies bled into the blackness of his mind. He was on his terrace, but there were no sounds coming off the bay. No rustling of the trees nearby or lapping of waves as they broke against the rocks. He turned to his right and saw her standing, back towards him, looking out to sea. Just as he motioned toward her, she stole a glance over her shoulder, looking into his eyes. Hers danced, smiling back at him, then gazed up at the sky behind him before her head turned around to look out toward the sea again.

His heart thudded violently as he realized this might be the last time he'd get to be with her this way. If Lu has anything to do with their lives, her dreams would not be private for a long time. Pushing down the words of his father and all care, he reached for her. His embrace was welcomed with her head resting on his chest. In this space, she could still hurt him, but at that moment, he felt no pain from her touch.

"Thank you," Mirah said just above a whisper.

"I wish I could have done more. Done something sooner."

"What you did was more than I could have hoped you'd do. You allowed yourself to be used by The Most High to set me free. For that, I am eternally grateful. Even in the strangest of circumstances, The Father makes away, using all that allow themselves to be used. Nephilim included."

"Our paths should never have crossed. I'm still trying to understand why he allowed it. Why he's allowing this moment; us here still sharing dreams."

"Hmmm, I've learned that he uses them to communicate with us and show us things we need to know for our life's journey. Maybe he has something even now to show you."

"Me. But I have no soul to redeem. My destiny is set, and my time is limited. No, all I can do is help you any way I can while at the same time, trying not to betray my kind. Still, you..."

Mirah turned then, looking up into the eyes of a being she'd always wondered if existed. She touched his face and felt him tremble slightly. His large yellow-gold rimmed, dark irises started back, reaching to the most hidden parts of her mind.

"I know you are also trying to protect me from something. Something that happened when I became free of Basielle."

Ayularc tried to deny it by shaking his head, but Mirah smiled and nodded that she understood he had good reasons. "No matter our fate, I believe The Father always had a good reason for us being thrown together. You didn't ask to be born, and everyone is ashamed of things done in their past. Make the best of the time you have left."

Ayularc felt an unbearable sadness rip away at his insides. The force caused his legs to buckle briefly. It was the words from his father that helped him not crumble before her.

Cherish the moment, my son. If you don't, you'll forever be tormented by not doing so. Still, you must learn to hide this from others because it will be used against you, especially in the days to come.

I don't....I don't know how to stop holding back! My heart is....it's...

It's feeling love, Ayularc. Love that only humans and The Most High can now fully appreciate. We, The Fathers, once knew such love, such intensity before our fall. It was like nothing else, the love we shared with him. Even in our current state, we still can relate to its pull, its fire. Let it consume you at least once, my son, my remnant of what I once held most dear.

Is this what my mother did to you? How she made you feel?

Her hold on me was different, but the effect, yes, it was the same intensity.

"I figured it out, you know." Mirah's words cut into his thoughts.

Ayularc looked at her with now questioning eyes. Still trying to contain himself. He managed to ask in a low, almost wavering voice, "Just what did your brilliant mind figure out?"

"How we can still meet in this space. Before it was the connection Basielle still held onto with you. Now that she is no longer a part of me, it means that you and I now have a covenant, somehow. The thing is, though, I'm not sure how it was initiated."

Exhaling and with a genuine smile, Ayularc did as his father encouraged; he let himself go. "I'm the one you can say that initiated it. The time I spent sharing dreams with you were refreshing to my constant life of pushing ahead. You helped me slow down. Appreciate the beauty of this realm the way I used to. Then, the longer you stayed here in this house with me, the more at ease you became around me, the door, if you will, opened—a door I gladly walked through."

"Does this mean I and my bloodline owe you as it would have Basielle?"

"No. I want nothing from you. Well, maybe the opportunity to visit with you from time to time—in the waking world that is."

"And what of visiting with me here in the dream world?" Mirah asked, saddened a little at the thought of no longer being able to take part in such a spiritual phenomenon.

"Hmmm, in this space, I can't promise I'll be able to restrain myself. You are all I could have ever wanted in a mate, and we know our kind can never be together. Besides, my fate is bad enough not to have extra added to it by The Most High for such defiance. Still, you make whatever time I have left bearable to live."

Before Mirah could respond, he pulled her close, burying his face into her hair, inhaling deeply, branding her scent to memory. Her body was stiff at first, then relaxed as if hugging someone she'd never see again.

Does she sense what is coming for us? Ayularc thought.

He squeezed a little harder and started to lift Mirah up; then, she was gone. *She's awake,* Ayularc thought, his heart hurting again.

You will survive this. You must. Ayularc's father said gently in his mind. He'd been reaching out, monitory Ayularc's emotions since their last mental conversation.

I know. It won't be easy, but I know.

This place is like a beehive. Word has already spread that she will be captured soon. It won't be pretty what they'll have done to her. Lu being Lu, will most likely require you to do the examinations.

I thought of that.

What will you do?

What I must. Whatever happens, know I love you. You have always done your best to shield me from dangers only The Fathers can wield. But this time, I do what needs to be done for my mother and the human part of me, which still hopes for an eternal future filled with life and joy. Even if that hope is fleeting. Don't worry, we'll see each other again.

Ayularc...., his father whispered his name in desperation before signing, acknowledging he understood and accepted whatever his son chose to do next.

Ayularc's eyes opened to again take in the beauty of the bay before him. He could hear Mirah moving about upstairs in her room. Remaining put, he decided to let her be, knowing she was too, replaying what had happened between them in the dream.

Master, dinner will be ready soon, as you requested, Flyenz advised.

Thanks, Ayularc replied, stretching his arms above his head, mentally preparing for the long night fast approaching.

He walked back to his lab and made back up copies of all the research he'd gathered in the recent months. Records of all the volunteers that had been delivered to the warehouse for DNA collection, new efficient ways to extract the DNA material, and a map of the area, marking where the volunteers were found. Other files containing formulas and new interfaces for the ships The Fathers used to enter the physical realm were also duplicated. He transferred the backed up data to sights across the world he'd been using for years. Safe holds that held a treasure trove which all but guaranteed his worth to the cause.

He stared at the downloading indicator bar on the computer screen. The data represented bodies that were drained of their blood and people who were kept alive at blood farms outside the city limits. Each megabyte of data represented a human's life source. But for him and his kind, it also meant survival. Nothing about life on Earth has changed much since before The Flood. The fittest and most ruthless survived. The computer beeped, indicating the backups were complete. Mindlessly, Ayularc shut the computer down and left the room, raising his hand to touch above the opening to seal it again. Only a few knew the lab existed, and he planned to keep it that way.

CHAPTER 23

Dinner was tasty as always, and Mirah laughed carefree at his many attempts of telling jokes. He wanted the time they had to be fun and light. Neither mentioned the dream they'd spent together. Each was holding it close, not wanting to part with the personal aspects it illuminated of one toward the other. The sun had started to set by the time they were done.

Mirah's cell phone rang, breaking the mood, and she thought to ignore it, but Ayularc insisted she answer. It was her boss wanting to know if she'd planned to make an appearance at the office anytime soon. With what was going on, Mirah all but forgot the place, and without being able to turn on her now bugged laptop, she'd not bothered to send him any emails. Quickly, she used the news about Tito being discovered as the reason she was not in the office. Feeling terrible, her boss told her to take all the time she needed and just email when she was ready to come back to work.

“I’m sorry. I should have let you use my computer to do your work on,” Ayularc mentioned once Mirah ended the call.

“Ahhh, that’s alright. I was not mentally able to do much work anyway. To be honest, work was the last thing I was focused on.” Mirah studied him, taking in his slight movements and eye contact avoidance. Something was weighing heavily on him. The sun was now completely set and the night sky, still filled with large clouds, managed to let a few stars twinkle. “It’s a beautiful night, all the same,” she probed, hoping to get a reaction from him.

He bit. “It is, isn’t it?” He took a deep breath and finally held her gaze. His eyes were tender, and his shoulders had relaxed. In a steady voice, he said, “Tonight, no matter what happens, I will protect you. I need you to trust me, Mirah. Can you do that? Can you trust me, completely, if only just this once?” His eyes now were serious, almost cold, but his voice was tender, pleading.

“I trust you, and I know you will do all you can to keep me safe.”

“Good, because they are coming. Not just for you but for me too.”

Mirah’s heart began to beat faster, and all she could do was start to pray. She held onto her faith that The

Most High was not going to let anything catch him by surprise. That even what the enemy was planning was all going to fulfill his purpose.

"Come, let's enjoy the sweet-smelling night air," Ayularc rose and reached for her hand. He led her out to the balcony of the dining area. A set of long lounge chairs with thick cushions welcomed them. The air was just the right temperature, too, at least for Ayularc.

Relaxing and stretched out, they both stared up at the sky. Much of the remaining time was spent talking about what Mirah wanted to do next. How she planned to continue helping families with missing people find closure and move on. She knew she'd never be able to tell them the truth as it would only cause them to inquire about things that would get them *disappeared.*

Ayularc just listened and swallowed hard to stop the rising anxiety building inside him. There was no way he would take such hopes from her. He let her plan and dream as he watched the skies for any changes.

⌘⌘⌘⌘⌘⌘

"The ships are loaded and ready."

"Good. I want her found, TONIGHT!" Lu replied to the head-bowed general.

"Where do you want her taken when found?"

"The rooms at the Rizeen Towers are ready. I'll meet you there."

Lu turned his back, signaling the conversation was over. He stared at nothingness and felt a prick of fear at his back. The entire series of incidents had him a little unraveled. He wondered if any others would develop such a connection with another human. How much of their plans could be compromised by someone exposing more than they should.

Has Ayularc exposed us? What secrets did his connection with this human reveal? Hmmm, the best way to tell is to have his hands be the ones taking her apart piece by piece. But what of The Creator's protection, his covering over her? Surely she has a strong relationship with him. Her level of spirituality would have to be high, very high. No matter, we have enough Humtracks on standby if needed to be added to any fight his remaining angels may try to start.

Lu turned to face The Fathers who had gathered, waiting to learn of what role they'd play that night if any. He slowly scanned the group, purposely letting his eyes pass Ayularc's father, only to quickly find him again. He flashed a cold smirk at him before speaking.

"Brothers, tonight we will begin the journey to unravel yet another mystery. One I have no doubt WILL be solved and provide us with insight *hopefully* of *The Creator's* plans. We know he's crafty and has not forgotten us. Still, we have an allotted time to rule, and with everything we possess, we will claim WHAT IS OURS!"

The group roared in agreement. The ground shook under their feet as electricity from their combined energies scattered in every direction. Humtracks in the distance, corralled in cages, barked and scratched, joining the chaotic chorus.

Ayularc's father did as the others, not giving away the dread he now felt full force. His thoughts were of his son and the hard choices he'd have to make soon. He cursed himself again for having let him be born; Ayularc, his pride, and cross to bear.

⌘⌘⌘⌘⌘⌘

The sounds of the night and cool breeze soon lulled Mirah to sleep. Even though she had slept off the effects of the drugs from earlier, her mind was tired, and soon she wasn't able to keep her eyes open. Ayularc let her drift off, retrieving a blanket to cover her. He wanted to stay there with her for as long as he could, cherishing every moment, watching her sleep. Not long after, he noticed a portion of the sky become pitch black, void of stars. His breath caught in his throat.

"FLYENZ!" Ayularc called out to his faithful assistant, who was lurking nearby on the rooftop.

"I see it, Master."

"Hold them off for as long as you can."

"Mirah. Mirah, wake up," Ayularc softly spoke, nudging her shoulders. "Mirah, you have to wake up now," he continued to urge.

"Ummm, I didn't think I could sleep again so soon. What time is it?" She asked, rubbing sleep from her eyes.

"Time for us to get you somewhere to rest. Come, please get up."

It was when she was on her feet and looking up at Ayularc she noticed something in the sky just over his head off in the distance over the mouth of the bay. A patch of black sky was sliced open and bright light pierced through it. She gasped as she thought of her dream months ago. She was living the moment in real-time. Mouth opened, she tried to speak, but Ayularc already knew what she was trying to say.

"Mirah, we can't stay here. WE HAVE TO GO!"

But she was cemented to the spot. Frozen, but not with fear. She looked in awe as the scene unfolded. Wide-eyed, full of questions as to how, why were they there? Ayularc was a Nephilim, yes, but this was a different level of crashing realities. The sky was opening up to another dimension right in front of her.

"MIRAH!"

"Where, where can we hide? I know you want to protect me, but you can't. I know this now," she said, reassuring him she was no longer afraid of what life had in store for her.

"We can resist, at least a little. Don't you want to live? To be free?"

"I have lived, and I've always been free. Don't you see? This is my life's journey. I just didn't want to face the fact that once your kind was searching for me, my time was limited. I had hoped for a miracle, but The Father showed me in a dream tonight just now that we all, even you, have a role to play." She smiled at him as he looked at her, still debating whether to pick her up and run or remain by her side until he no longer could.

Defeated, he sighed and pulled her close. Little pricks of energy tazed his body, but he didn't care. He didn't want her to see the Humtracks he could hear and smell on the cloaked ship now slipping through the tear in the sky. He wanted to shield her from unnecessary horror about to be unleashed.

The ship was now hovering in the sky. Ayularc felt the restlessness of those inside it. Mirah's attention was still being held by the tear in the sky. The ship's cloaking made it so no human eye could easily detect it was there. But those on the ship would be seen once they exited.

"So the dream I had.."

"This is the beginning of it," Ayularc finished.

"These clouds that have been hanging around?"

"Ships for when the open take over begins. Tonight is another test run, but you are the sole human target."

A shriek and snarling sounded from the sky, and moments later, tall beings, taller than Ayularc, appeared to walk on air. Mirah couldn't make out any distinctive features, just their black silhouettes. With a turn of their heads, they looked toward the space from where they appeared. Next, streams of multi-leg creatures scurried out and free falled to the ground. All landing in the bay's water, swimming feverously towards the shore, towards Ayularc's house.

Horror and awe masked Mirah's face as she continued to watch, paralyzed. Ayularc grabbed her face, forcing her to look at him now, pleading with his eyes for her not to break his stare. She didn't. The reality of the moment finally sinking in.

With a raspy voice, Ayularc spoke loud enough for her to hear over the sound of the Humtracks approaching. “I said I’d protect you, and I keep my word. You are burned to my mind, my spirit, Mirah Dyrsen Maurez. Never have I met a human, a female like you, and I fear fate will not let me do so again.”

Mirah reached up and ran fingers through his flaxen hair, now falling like curtains to the sides of his face as he bent down looking at her. If he were a normal human man, he would have long won her heart. But he wasn’t, and this was no fairy tale book. This was the reality of the world which many soon would discover. Her eyes started to tear up, and her mouth quiver. Salty drops fell to her cheeks when she blinked, and like a dam breaking, Ayularc’s humanity flooded him.

He gently kissed the droplets as fast as they fell. The shrieking and snarling of the Humtracks continued to get closer. He estimated they would be upon them in under a minute.

“I’m sorry. I’m so sorry,” he mumbled between capturing each tear. “I will never let them, have you. I can take a lot, but to witness you being examined, taken apart, that I don’t think I would recover from.”

“Ayularc, there is nothing you can do to stop this. I’m terrified, yes, but I know soon I’ll be with my savior. My spirit will finally find rest. Know that I don’t blame you for anything that may happen next. You kept your word, and I was safe. This is just how my story ends in this life. I’m kinda eager to begin the next one.” Mirah did her best to keep a look of hope on her face as she tried to wash away his guilt.

With a sad smile, he rose his head and looked at her. Her beauty and spirit stole his breath, and without another thought, he claimed her lips. Forbidden or not, he was already damned, and he knew the moment wouldn't come again. He drank in all she would let him have, her lips parting, allowing him free reign.

In her mind, Mirah knew she wouldn't live long enough to face the consequences of the covenant their kiss made. It was all she could do to not run as she too could now hear the chilling sounds of the creatures. Shivers ran up and down her spine as she let Ayularc's kiss attempt to drag her focus to anything but what was happening around her.

Sudden intense pain in her chest caught her by surprise. Ayularc continued to kiss her as the agony spread out toward her shoulders. Bile and blood shot up her throat and sputtered out her mouth. Only then did he release her just enough to see her face.

She smiled through the discomfort as crimson fluid continued to drip from her lips. Mirah shook her head as Ayularc continued to state how sorry he was. It was the only way he could save her from the torture he knew would be hers.

"Thank...you," Mirah sputtered, her breathing became labored.

"I'm so sorry, Mirah. I'm so sorry," Ayularc said as his own eyes watered for the first time in years.

By the time her last breath escaped, Humtracks had gathered at their feet. Two of Lu's generals approached, one keeping his eye on Flyenz, who had long jumped down from the rooftop, and emerged to stand now behind Mirah's lifeless body. He helped Ayularc keep it standing by supporting her back. With a command, the Humtracks crouched, stopping their shrieks and snarling.

"We're here to take you both to the Rizeen Towers," the general closest to Ayularc said. He peered over Ayularc's shoulder, seeing the now dead Mirah being hoisted up. "Our orders were for her to be taken alive; what did you do?!"

"I set her free," Ayularc said, his voice strengthening as he assessed the situation. "Let Lu know that I will be happy to provide something of greater value than this human female."

"You can tell him yourself. One way or another, you're both coming with us!" The general continued, now signaling for the Humtracks to return to the ship, currently visible silently hovering just a feet away from where they stood.

Ayularc handed Flyenz Mirah's body, then turned to face the general. His height did not intimidate Ayularc, whose face had now become hardened. Before he could respond to the question, another tear formed. Ayularc smirked slightly as he saw Lu step through the tear in the night sky. He figured such a prize Lu would not easily trust anyone to collect. He knew this one's ego well—he had planned on it being just the way it was, fragile and inflated.

Without a word, Lu walked over to inspect Mirah's body. He sighed and dropped his head a little, then slowly raised it again, saying, "What did you hope to gain by killing her, Ayularc? You must know that alive or dead; she holds much value to us."

"That may be so, but at least she wouldn't be a homing beacon to our location dead. If she was able to connect with me, who knows what her spirit was able to transmit to The Light?"

"THAT was not a choice for you alone to make!" Lu took a deep breath then exhaled slowly. Ayularc could see his mind trying to figure the next move to salvage the situation. Noting it as the perfect opportunity to show his hand, Ayularc took one step closer to Mirah's body.

"If you would concede to allowing me to remain here and continue my work, I believe I can duplicate the process that made her and I connect." Lu's eyebrows raised. He licked his lips as if trying to catch a tasty morsel before it dropped. Ayularc continued, laying it on thick enough to give Lu little wiggle room. "I have documented proof and inside, first-hand experience of what it would take to make this benefit the plan. I understand you've already placed ships in position. Imagine having thousands like her become hosts for thousands still trapped in The Void. Flesh suits take time and labor to produce. This alternative could overnight increase our numbers in the physical world, while flesh suites are being made for long term use."

Lu glanced from Ayularc to Mirah's body then back again. The sparkle in his eyes and smile forming at his lips told Ayularc he might have succeeded in escaping The Void himself. "One thing though, I will need to destroy this body, just to be sure there is no way it can be used to reveal our location to The Light."

"On that, we both can agree. However, I shall be sure it is destroyed. Call it my assurance that whatever you're scheming doesn't backfire, and I have to face the brunt of the wrath of my brothers," Lu cooed, signally with his hand for the two generals to collect Mirah's body and board their ship with it.

Knowing he had no choice but to let Lu take Mirah's body, Ayularc nodded to Flyenz to not resist. He clenched his teeth together as they picked her up. The soothing voice of his father stopped him just as he was about to reach for her hair for the last time.

Don't you dare move! You've saved her from unthinkable pain and suffering. That's all you could have done. Remember, she has long since left that body and is now in Paradise. She is free, safe. You kept your promise, son.

Ayularc didn't reply. He just stood there, trying to keep his breathing even and show no emotion. As Lu followed the others to the hovering ship, he paused and slightly turned his head to say,

"Well played. Like father, like son."

The words caught Ayularc off guard, his face confirming it. By now, Lu had turned completely around, facing him as he hovered mid-air near the hovering now re-cloaked ship.

"He didn't tell you it all, I see. Well, your father was mortified that your mother had conceived, no matter how careful he'd tried to be with her. The fate that awaited her during childbirth was one he couldn't bear to witness."

Still uncertain where Lu's story was headed, Ayularc swallowed hard, bracing himself for what he knew would be another gut punch, and his gut was already sore from the recent events of the night.

"Yes, your father cared deeply for your mother, so much that he cut you himself from her body seconds after he smothered her as she gasped and screamed in pain. He always would say it was the least painful thing he could do for her, given the circumstances. Still, it may have saved your mother further moments of agony, but your father—well, he has carried that pain from the day you were born.

Interesting to see how even in our fallen state and through procreation with women, some traits still pass along our bloodline. Take advice from me, Ayularc, don't get attached to them, *any* of them. They are prey, and we are the hunters." With that, Lu walked backward into the ship then disappeared as the cloaked door closed.

Ayularc stood there, statue still until he watched the ship return through the tear in the sky. He knew they'd go to the Rizeen Towers to dispose of Mirah's body in the newly renovated labs there. It didn't matter. He still had one more move to make. Climbing onto the rooftop of his home, with Flyenz following behind, Ayularc had a clear view of the building sticking up in the city skyline.

He waited for several minutes, and using his unnatural sight abilities, spotted the cloaked ship hovering a few feet away from the roof. He waited until he could see Mirah's body being taken into the building through a rooftop access door. With the dial of Mirah's cell phone number, Ayularc watched as a large fiery ball of orange and black shot up into the night's sky, seconds after the first ring.

Sirens blared in the distance moments later. Black smoke now billowed from the building. Ayularc and Flyenz stood in silence. No words or shared thoughts between them. With the building destroyed, Lu would have no choice but to return to the spirit realm. The loss of the Humtracks and the ship would surely piss him off, but he and his generals would survive the blast.

Ayularc's cell phone began to vibrate in his pant pocket. Without checking the caller ID, he answered, "Yes?"

"Sir, the Rizeen....the Rizeen is...gone. Blown up!"

"Relax. It was bound to happen with the faulty gas lines running through it. If the other investors refused my advice to repair them properly, why are you stressing out over it?"

"But Sir, you too have much to lose by its destruction!"

"I do? Really? Hmmm, I see it as me just gaining more than you can ever imagine."

"Sir?"

“Nevermind. I have to go, but do let me know when the other investors take my recent buyout offer, will you?”

“Yes, yes, of course, sir. Good night.”

Ayularc ended the call. Without ceremony, he and Flyenz left the roof and went inside. Flyenz could sense Ayularc wished to be alone. So without a word he saw himself out the front door.

Ayularc slowly walked around the main living space. The house felt empty without her. Each room still had some of her scent, but it was fading. He took the stairs to the second floor two by two until almost breathlessly, he stood in the spare bedroom, her room.

Mirah’s scent, strong in the space, engulfed him like an invisible net. He fell onto the bed, grabbing the pillows inhaling deeply. He remained that way until sunrise, falling in and out of sleep. His dreams, though, were filled only with past memories of the time before The Flood. Ayularc searched everywhere for her in his dreams, but she was gone. Totally and completely gone. He finally pulled himself off the bed and went to his room to change clothes.

Today was as good as any for a family reunion. With little effort, he cut through the air in his bedroom and stepped into the spirit realm. His father stood off a little ways, waiting for him. Not much was said as they walked along, going nowhere in particular. Ayularc just needed relatability right then. Someone who could understand his pain. The visit lasted most of the day, and when Ayularc finally was ready to speak, his words were that of a question.

"What do I do now, father?"

"You live out your days, making the most of them."

"How do I live out my days when the best I've ever known is gone?"

"One breath at a time, son. One breath at a time."

TURN THE PAGE

TO CHECK OUT

BOOK II

PREY OR BE PRAY II

CHAPTER 1

Ayularc woke with a fright. Even for him, the visions were so real, tangible. He could feel the change in temperature as day and night rotated. Her scent. The tonal inflections of her voice. The touch of skin, warm and subtle. All of which belonged to a woman that captured his breath even now. Mirah. He raised a hand to his forehead, forcing the memories to surface. Mirah, Mirah Dryson. Daylight would soon bathe the exterior walls of his house. As much as Ayularc wanted to relive the thoughts now flooding his mind, he pushed himself off the bed and started his day.

Mentally, he made a list of things he wanted to confirm. There was a lot he needed to decipher, and the list of questions kept getting longer. Either way, Ayularc expected there would be joy or a haunting of his peace at the end of his investigation. Glimpses continued to flash in his mind of all he'd seen. Experiences that gave him mostly a warm sensation, then at others, ones of horrible dread. Shaking his head, he let his eyes scan the clothes hanging in the master bedroom closet.

Arrrg, no use trying to get anything else done until I solve this riddle, Ayularc thought to himself, as his eyes landed on a pair of black denim jeans and a white long sleeve pullover.

He laid the clothes out on his bed and then proceeded to the shower. As if on autopilot, he reached for the bottle of shampoo, just as he had countless times before. The rush of the scent from the thick liquid sent him mentally back to a prior vision. Even now, he remembered how in that vision the notes of cedar's sweet citrus, rosemary's minty-pine, and soft musk of vanilla swirled around his freshly washed hair.

Quickly, Ayularc washed his hair and showered. Stepping out of the shower, his wet feet made quick of the length of the room to the counter. Reaching for his cell phone, he searched for a name. Damp fingers danced over the slick screen protector. As soon as he'd entered the name, the search results showed. Mirah Dryson, reporter at Cityscape Daily. Ayularc clicked on the first listed link, which took him to a page on the Cityscape Daily's website. It was one that listed the personnel. A long index finger swiped upward twice before his hand paused a few inches away from the cell phone. There, staring back at him, was a face he could not have imagined. Eyes that bore through him even now, encased in the screen of his cell phone. Her name and position were just under the image. This time, Ayularc read the words out loud, as if that would make the confusion of information his mind was attempting to sort out happen any faster.

"Mirah Dryson, reporter at Cityscape Daily. Mirahhhh," her name trailed off as he slowly placed the cell phone on the bathroom counter.

Raising his head, Ayularc gazed at his reflection in the mirror that was almost clear of the fog his shower had caused. "What in the world? Why is this woman in my head, my dreams? And how is it that my ex-wife is mixed up in all of this, this, this complete mind trip? But I killed her? This Mirah Dryson. Didn't I? Arrrg, I can hardly tell what's real from a dream right now!

"Flyenz!"

"Yes, Master," Ayularc's assistant replied as the two of them spoke telepathically.

"Find out all you can about Mirah Dryson. She's a reporter at the Cityscape Daily. The office is downtown and if she's indeed still working there, deliver a written message for her to meet me this afternoon around 1:30 pm at Cannes Café. Add my cell number to the note as well."

"Yes, Master. As you wish."

“Any updates on last night’s arrival of new blood donors?”

“All accounted for, Master. Our sources have been keeping up with the requested quota.”

“Humm, yes, I suspect they will. Money and a false sense of power, can be great motivators for humans.”

“Yes, Master. Do you need anything else before I head downtown?”

“No thanks. I shall be out of my office today, so call me the moment you have delivered the message. And do wait to make sure she reads it, will you?”

“Of course, Master.”

⌘⌘⌘⌘⌘⌘

Piercing pain yanked at Mirah’s chest. Even in her current state, she tried to be free of it, but nothing she did caused the pain to let up. Moistened bed sheets had twisted around her legs as she kicked and moaned until a scream escaped between parched lips. Like a pulled back metal coil, she sprang up in the middle of the bed. Left hand still in a fist as she tried to press against her chest, as if that would keep her heart in place. Panting now, she searched the room, confirming that this time she was wide-awake. Licking her lips, her tongue caught droplets of sweat, which had snaked down her face. Mirah continued to take in her surroundings.

"What was that? God, I thought I was awake! What in the—how could that have all been a dream or vision? Okay, Father, you need to explain that one to me. And why did that man shove his hand in my chest and..."

Mirah gasped. Her eyes looked beyond the foot of her bed, as if watching the last memory replay itself. She wasn't now recalling the man, whose face was still blurry, but the black ugly dogs. No, they weren't dogs, but that's how her brain was registering them. She let her mind bring more details forward and then she saw the generals and what looked like a tear in the night's sky.

"What? How? Okay, seriously, Father, I need answers and I need them now!"

Before Mirah could get any revelation about what she had seen in her dreams, the meeting reminder notification sounded on her cell phone. She had just over two hours to be dressed, at work, and ready to pitch her latest story to her editor. Dream, vision, whatever, was going to have to wait. She was just happy to still be in the land of the living, but from what she just experienced, she wasn't sure if the land was only for "the living."

Get Book II today.

ACKNOWLEDGMENTS

Thank you Heavenly Father for giving me the focus and determination to finish this book. I would also like to thank you for all the wonderful story ideas, which I pray help to bring awareness of your love and mercy to others.

A special shoutout to all of the Beta Readers who gave great feedback and suggestions which helped to make this books completion possible. Also, for all who support my works THANK YOU from the bottom of my heart. You are the ones I think of when creating plot twisting reads! You are appreciated and I read all of your precious reviews, so please do leave one.

If you would like to be an Alpha or Beta Reader for my current works in progress, message me on Facebook, Instagram or Twitter.

Facebook @AuthorZitaGrant
Instagram & Twitter @ZitaG_Author

Subscribe to Zita's website to get the latest book information. You can also request to be an Alpha, or Beta Reader. Oh, and you could win free gifts too.

Website: ZitaGrant.com

ABOUT THE AUTHOR

Zita Grant is an author, publisher, three-time-startup CEO and founder in both the beauty and tech industries. Necessity continues to be the drive behind the nonfiction books she writes. Those currently published, contain sought after content that increases daily her diverse worldwide readership and following. The production of fictional stories helps balance Zita's numerous creative ideas. She has also successfully coached writers who've later become published authors, and entrepreneurs who have achieved both business growth and development, resulting from her business acumen.

When not working in tech coding, creating cinematic book trailers (ZitaCodes.tech) or overseeing the operations of 2 Tigers LLC, Zita enjoys devouring books from her regularly growing library, watching a movie, or enjoying the outdoors.

Zita is always open to collaboration, so if you are an author or work in publishing, connect with her and see how she can assist with your next project.